Another book by Jacqueline Roy

FAT CHANCE

Jacqueline Roy

A Daughter Like Me

PUFFIN BOOKS

For Naomi Roy, with love

PUFFIN BOOKS

Published by the Penguin Group
Penguin Books Ltd, 27 Wrights Lane, London W8 5TZ, England
Penguin Books USA Inc., 375 Hudson Street, New York, New York 10014, USA
Penguin Books Australia Ltd, Ringwood, Victoria, Australia
Penguin Books Canada Ltd, 10 Alcorn Avenue, Toronto, Ontario, Canada M4V 3B2
Penguin Books (NZ) Ltd, 182–190 Wairau Road, Auckland 10, New Zealand

Penguin Books Ltd, Registered Offices: Harmondsworth, Middlesex, England

First published by Viking 1996
Published in Puffin Books 1997
3 5 7 9 10 8 6 4 2

Filmset in Bembo

Made and printed in England by Clays Ltd, St Ives plc

One

My strongest feeling about the new house was one of disappointment. It was so different from the way I had imagined it.

It was the kind of disappointment you feel when you're absolutely counting on something to go right to make up for everything that's going wrong. I'd thought that moving to London would change things for the better, but as soon as I saw the house I knew it could only make them worse.

Even now, I can smell the mustiness of the place. I remember thinking there was probably a body or two buried in the cellar, it was that kind of house. The carpet was worn and faded, as if someone had tried to scrub a sinister stain out of it and hadn't quite managed to rub all the nastiness out of the fibres. The paint on the skirting boards was chipped and flaking. There was a damp patch on the ceiling and a cracked window pane in the living-room. I didn't say anything because I'm the brave one in the family, but I couldn't stop worrying that someone would break into the house through that window when we were least expecting it. I felt so jumpy I was scared that one of the others would notice, but of course they were too wrapped up in their own worries to care about what was bothering me.

I let the box of books I was carrying hit the floor with a loud crash. That woke them up a bit. Ella jumped and said, 'Be careful, Bess,' in her usual superior way.

I perched on top of the box and said, 'I don't see why we have to live in this house anyway,' although of course, I knew perfectly well. Dad was out of work and there wasn't any money. We'd come to London because jobs were easier to find down south than they were in Leeds. And because it was falling down, the house was cheap and we could afford it – *just*.

'This house is junk,' I said, pushing home the point. I knew I should just shut up and get on with things the way that Ella was doing, but I couldn't sit on myself that hard. She gave me a look which let me know I was being a pain but all she said was, 'It's not that bad. Why can't you be more like Jude? She isn't complaining, she's trying to help.'

There's nothing worse than being compared unfavourably to a younger sister, especially when the sister in question is only six years old. I gave Jude one of my looks of contempt and said, 'I could have carried that box here in half the time. She drops everything anyway.'

As if to order, Jude lost her hold on the box of soft toys she was carrying. Two chimpanzees, a one-eared zebra, three large teddies and a turquoise elephant tumbled on to the mat. Jude tossed them back in the box and continued her journey up the narrow staircase. 'I don't play with these any more,' she confided as she went. 'It's just hard to chuck them. I mean, you don't get rid of your friends just because they're too old or because you're too old, do you? It would be cruel.'

Ella thought Jude was cute when she said things like that, but I wasn't impressed. She was an extremely irritating child, and big brown eyes and a sweet smile and African curls that clustered round her mid-brown face cut no ice with me. I knew what she was doing anyway. She was trying to be grown-up. Dad's big phrase of the moment was, 'You're all going to have to be very grown-up about this.' He said it every time anything went wrong, and as things had gone wrong pretty often these past few months, we'd heard it a whole lot more than we would have liked.

Ella took advantage of Jude's absence to tell me I shouldn't have brought my train set. You're probably wondering what a girl of eleven would want with one, but I liked the boredom of it. You see, I have a very lively mind. I'm such a quick thinker that every now and then I need to take some time to catch up with myself. The train set had been Dad's when he was a boy, and I'd got pretty attached to it. Watching those trains going round and round in their slow, methodical way was very soothing, and it always settled me down, got me thinking good, interesting thoughts. I wasn't giving it away, not for anyone. I didn't care whether there was room or not. I said some of this to Ella, who tried to smooth things over as she always did.

'It's not me who wants you to get rid of it, it's Dad. You don't want him to get upset, do you?'

There wasn't really an answer to this, although I was at the point where I didn't much care whether Dad was upset or not. I went upstairs to my room and looked out of the window on to the large, old building opposite. A lorry was backing into its yard.

Jude and Ella came in without bothering to knock. I glared at them, but they didn't seem to notice. 'It makes a lot of noise, doesn't it?' Jude said.

'It'll go on all night. We won't get any sleep. Told you this was a dump,' I answered.

'It'll be all right,' said Ella.

I drew a circle on the window-pane. Rivulets of condensation trickled down it.

Jude's eyes were still on the lorry. 'It's big. I'd like to drive one some day.'

Another one of Jude's so-called cute remarks. I couldn't help trying to deflate her. 'Well, I wouldn't. They're noisy and ugly, and having to live opposite will drive us crazy. You'd think Dad could have found somewhere better for us to live than this. I think he's gone funny.'

As soon as it was out, I wished I hadn't said it, not because I was being noble and knew I'd just scared Jude, but because I'd scared myself. It was one of those secret fears that are much more likely to come true once you've said them than if you don't. I wanted to take it back, but it was too late. Ella looked miserable. I waited for her to say that it wasn't true and Dad was fine, but there was only silence. Life was verminous sometimes. It was a good word, that. I'd found it in a book the day before and I'd been storing it up for an appropriate moment, but I didn't say it out loud just then because it was too unfamiliar and I didn't want it to come out wrong and make me look stupid. I remember once, when I was just a little kid, I said, 'That tree has ravenous branches.' I'm not even sure what I really meant, I've forgotten all the details, but I do remember all the grown-ups laughing at me as if I was stupid, so I'm very careful now.

Ella said, 'Dad's fine, he's done all right,' but she was about five minutes too late, and I knew she thought he was on another planet too.

'Dad's fine, he's done all right,' echoed Jude, another one of her irritating habits.

I said, 'You call this all right?' and gestured round me at the house. I knew I ought to stop saying all this negative stuff, but I couldn't help myself, I was too utterly fed up. Mum used to say that my mouth ran away with me, and she was right, it was like a huge ugly roller coaster that hauled you along with it, up and down and round and round, and once you were on, you couldn't get off again.

'I like it,' said Ella, but she was too slow again. You have to lie quickly for it to be convincing.

'I like it too,' said Jude, and looking back, I think she probably did. You know what six-year-olds are like, they have no taste in anything.

'Well, I hate it,' I said. 'I never wanted to come here anyway. Why does everything bad have to happen to us?'

Ella opened her mouth to tell me to shut up, but she suddenly closed it again. I knew that she'd seen I was trying not to cry and that made me crosser than ever.

'Dad's home!' said Jude, and she and Ella ran to the door.

'Not so fast,' Dad said, as Jude tumbled towards him. He put out his hand to hold her back as if he didn't want her near him. He went into the kitchen with the bags of groceries, and we followed. I was hoping that he'd brought back a treat to celebrate the move, or at least to make it seem more bearable. I picked up one of the bags and rummaged inside it, but there was nothing of any interest so I started on another.

Dad just said, 'Why haven't you finished unpacking your toys?' in a cold, flat voice.

'Sorry, Dad,' said Ella.

I pulled out a packet of sausages. 'What's this?' I asked.

'What's it look like?' said Dad.

'I hate sausages, they're disgusting, you don't know what's in them.'

'Too bad. We can't afford to be picky any more.'

'Life's a B –' I began, but he interrupted me.

'Don't even think about saying that. It's one of the ugliest expressions.'

'This house is ugly, but we've still got to live in it. Sausages are ugly, but we still have to eat them.'

'Shut up, Bess.'

I can't stand it when people tell me I'm not

allowed to say what I think. It's a civil liberty and the right of every child. 'I wish I didn't have to live with you!' I shouted at the top of my voice.

'My wish is just the same as yours!' he shouted back.

I shot out of the room and upstairs then, pounding on the staircase as hard as I could. I wanted him to call after me to show me that he understood the way I felt, but there was only the sound of Ella opening and shutting kitchen cupboards as she put the groceries away. I flung myself on my bed. I didn't want any of them then, I decided, I wanted to be on my own. Nobody understood, they never ever knew what I meant about anything. I wanted to grind them into dust and hoover it up. I smiled to myself as I pictured the faded yellow bag puffed up with their remains. Then I crept out of my room and sat on the stairs, just out of sight. They were talking about me. I'd guessed they would be.

'She's just being stupid,' said Jude, all smug and sweet. She'd be the first in that hoover bag.

I could hear Ella continuing to tidy the kitchen. I pictured the scene. It wasn't like the kitchen we used to have at home. Here, the tap dripped constantly. The cooker had two rings that wouldn't light. One of the cupboard doors had a hinge missing so the door swung out crookedly. No one worth their salt would live in a place like this.

'She's upset, she doesn't know what's going on,' said Dad after a while. His pauses irritated me, I like things to move fast.

'What is going on?' asked Jude.

Dad gave a laugh that went on for a long, long time. 'How would I know?' he said eventually.

Everyone fell silent. I wriggled uncomfortably. I hated it when he laughed like that. It wasn't proper laughter, the kind you get when something's really funny, it was the sort of laughter that was empty of happiness and meant something else entirely. I don't think any of us knew what to do when Dad was in one of these moods. I remember thinking that if Mum had been there, she would have made things better, but we didn't really know how.

'I could make a cup of tea,' said Ella at last, breaking the silence that was so dense now you could almost touch it. I heard the gas ring give a little pop as Ella lit it with a match. She was so adult in some ways and such a kid in others. I loved her and hated her at exactly the same time.

'This door's so ruddy irritating!' Dad snapped, and then there was a crash.

I jumped, and came running down the stairs. 'What was that?' I said in a fright.

'The cupboard door came off,' said Ella.

'Dad kicked it,' added Jude.

I looked at him and he turned red, just like a child of Jude's age.

Momentarily, I felt sorry for him. 'I thought it was a bomb,' I said. I was trying to make a joke of it to save his embarrassment.

'Don't be silly,' he replied.

I looked at the floor. I'd only said it because

I wanted to help. Why couldn't he understand?

Jude tried to change the subject. Sometimes she was quite sharp for an infant. 'We've nearly done the unpacking now, honest, Dad. I took my toys up to Ella's and my room.'

Dad didn't answer. He was staring absently out of the kitchen window. I tugged on his sleeve. 'There are lorries over there,' I said, trying to get his attention.

'They'll keep us awake.'

'That's just what I said,' I answered, pleased that we were on the same wavelength again. 'Ella thought it would be all right.'

'Don't worry about it, Dad,' said Ella, handing him a mug of tea. He took it without answering. He didn't even look at her.

Suddenly, I wanted to run up to my room again, but I was scared to leave, so we all stood there in silence, as if we were waiting for something to happen. Then Ella opened a packet of biscuits, the plain, dry sort that certainly aren't any kind of treat, but she couldn't find a plate to put them on because they were still packed in the boxes. I realized then that it would be weeks before things got back to normal and couldn't help wondering if a normal life was even possible any more.

I decided that it was stupid to stay downstairs when everything was so horrible, and then it came to me that the reason I couldn't just go was that I was worried in case Dad kicked something or lost control of himself in some other, more scary way. But then, I couldn't keep an eye on him all the time, it was impossible, and besides, I needed some time to myself. Ella would help him if he needed it. She was better at it anyway.

It was a relief to escape to my room. It was the size of a cupboard, but at least it was mine. Ella should have had it, being the eldest, but I'd nagged Dad into giving it to me. I suppose I shouldn't have, but I'd have gone crazy sharing with Jude, and Ella was much better at putting up with things like that. I'd decided that my need was greater than hers.

I felt in my pocket for the small red car I'd carried around with me since I was a little kid. No one knew I still had it. It felt comforting and familiar in all the strangeness. As I pulled my hand out again, a crumpled bit of paper came with it. I smoothed it out and began to read, but I was interrupted by a scuffling outside the door. It was only Ella. 'Can't you knock?' I growled at her, as she pushed the door open with her foot.

'My hands are full. I brought your books, you left them in the hall. Dad's doing his nut.'

'So what's new?' I said. Still, it wasn't Ella's fault, so I added a curt thanks.

'What are you doing?' she asked.

'What's it look like?'

She sat beside me on the bed. 'You're reading that leaflet,' she said.

'Clever!' I said sarcastically. I was hardly ever nice to Ella.

'Where did you get it from?'

'It was stuffed in the letter-box this morning.'

Ella took the leaflet from me and did a better job of smoothing it out. All the words were legible now. CLUB FOR TWELVES TO FOURTEENS AT CHESTNUT HALL, FRIDAYS, 5 P.M. TILL 8.

'You aren't twelve yet,' said Ella.

'I will be soon, and I look twelve. Anyway, who's going to ask?'

'Someone will, I bet you anything. I could go though.'

'You couldn't go without me, you wouldn't know what to do.'

I could tell by Ella's face that she knew this was true. She was hopeless when it came to meeting new people, she was so shy, she hardly said a word. I never have a problem with that kind of thing. I decided to use my powers of persuasion. If you could get Ella on your side, you were half-way there because Dad reckoned she was responsible and she could usually get him to agree to things. So I said, 'We don't know anyone in London, we don't have a single friend. If we go to this club, we could meet people, find out stuff.'

'I don't want to meet people,' said Ella.

'You're so boring.'

'I'm not.'

'You are, take it from me.' Ella didn't answer this so I decided to try coaxing – it often worked with Ella where goading failed. 'It would be fun, I know it would, you'd like it once you got used to it. Dad would be happier if he thought we were liking it here.'

'You don't care how Dad feels.'

'I do, you know I do. He'll calm down if he thinks we're OK and making friends.'

'Maybe, but he probably won't want us to go. He thinks London's dangerous, much worse than Leeds. He won't like us going somewhere he doesn't know.'

I screwed the leaflet into a little ball and flung it across the room. 'I wish we could go back home,' I said.

'Me too,' said Ella. Then she added, 'Bess, do you think Dad's OK?'

'I don't know. What do you think?'

Ella fidgeted with the tassels on my bedspread. She put on her responsible expression, the one which said she was the oldest and should take care not to frighten the little ones. Eventually, she spoke. 'I think that if we try not to be horrible about this move and try not to fight or be mean to him, Dad might get happier.'

Of course, I realized then I'd handed Ella the chance to give me a lecture. You'd have thought I'd have known better. But she was right in a way, so I said, 'We could try I suppose, but I do hate it when we have to keep pretending everything's all right and we don't mind stuff that we do mind. I forget to do it all the time.'

Ella felt in the pocket of her jeans. 'I've got a bit of chocolate. I was saving it but we could have it now.'

I suppose I should have had more pride than to take a bribe, but if Ella really thought I wouldn't do it any other way it seemed only right to humour her. I took a large piece.

Once Ella had gone, I retrieved the orange leaflet and examined it again. It would be good to meet people, make some friends and stop feeling so cut off from all the things I knew. Suddenly I thought of Mum, but I quickly brushed the memory aside. It was over. Things would never be the same, so there was no point in thinking about it. How long was it before you stopped minding? A year? Two years? Never? Mum had been dead for ten months, and the really terrible sadness had faded, but it wasn't all right yet, not nearly. None of us talked about her much any more, we just couldn't, I suppose, especially Dad.

Ever since I could remember, he'd had moods, really bad ones, and he'd get sadder and sadder and gradually stop doing things. First of all, he'd stop smiling, then he'd stop doing things around the house. Then he'd stop working. Then he'd stop talking and eating and he'd want to stay in bed all the time. It was depression, but not the everyday kind of being miserable, it was much, much worse than that. Mum used to say it was like being in a huge dark hole that swallowed you up. It was an illness, she'd said, and you had to take pills for it. I wished Mum was there then because she'd always managed to get Dad out of his holes, no matter how deep they'd become. But there didn't seem to be anything Ella or I could do and things were getting worse, they definitely were, anyone could see that, even a blindfolded cat with a wooden leg.

I tired to imagine such a cat and the thought cheered me up even though I was so miserable. I put the corner of the leaflet into my mouth. Orange things ought to have an orange taste, but they didn't, they were disappointing. Most things were disappointing, come to think of it. I got under the bedclothes. It was dark down there, and very like being in a hole. I thought of Dad then, and I couldn't help thinking about Mum too. I cried for a moment, but I didn't want to cry, so I opened a book and began to read it furiously, shutting out the world.

Two

I was awake early next morning. It's always hard to sleep in new surroundings, and it was only the second night. Just as I had predicted, lorries were moving in and out of the yard at the back of the house. I pulled the bedclothes over my head and pretended I couldn't hear them. I didn't want to be aware of anything, I wanted to believe I was there by myself. In the old house there had been lots of space, places to run around in. And when I'd wanted to be quiet, there'd been places to hide in. Nothing was private in this new house, but at least I didn't have to share a bedroom.

I held my wrist up to look at my watch, forgetting that I hadn't been able to wear it for days. The battery had run down, and Dad said it would cost too much money to replace it. It's funny how much you take for granted. Before Mum died, things like that had been there for the asking.

The window was situated just above the bed, so I sat up and pulled back the curtains, hoping to tell the time by the strength of the daylight. At least the sun was out. I could tell it would be cold though, because my toes were like ice cubes and my feet are never wrong about the weather. I wondered what we'd be doing that day. Back in Leeds, there were things to do come rain or shine. You could go round to see friends or wander through the shopping centre or go to see a film. Here in South London everything was unfamiliar, and I knew there wouldn't be the pleasure of doing my favourite things over and over again the way I'd done back home. I still thought of Leeds as home, even though I was actually a Londoner by birth. We'd all gone north a long time ago, when I'd been six or seven, and I didn't remember anything about London now, except that there were huge shops in Oxford Street where you could visit Santa Claus at Christmas.

Mum had been great at Christmas time. She'd always managed to get us exactly what we wanted even when all the shops seemed to have sold out. She'd always made the Christmas pudding in advance like you were supposed to do and she'd cooked the turkey while Dad did the vegetables. Then, once we'd eaten and the washing-up was done, she'd played games with us for the rest of the day. But last Christmas had been different. Two days before, there'd been a row, something to do with Dad not trying hard enough to help himself out of one of his bad patches. Mum had got in the car in a temper and had driven off. Then we'd got a phone call. Mum had been in an accident and the car was a write-off. Dad had rushed to the hospital to be with Mum, and he'd stayed even on Christmas Day. We'd spent the time at a neighbour's house. I remembered how sure I'd been that Mum would wake up that day. It was Christmas, nothing bad happened then, it was a time when everything came right. I'd sat by the phone in the hall, pretending to play with an assortment of pocket games so that no one would know I was waiting. In the evening, a call had come from Dad. Mum had never regained consciousness.

For weeks after, I'd asked myself a whole list of questions, which I'd gone over silently again and again. Why hadn't Mum woken up? Hadn't she known how much we'd needed her? Although I knew Mum couldn't have wanted to leave us, I was angry just the same. She shouldn't have gone out in a temper. If she could have concentrated better on her driving maybe it wouldn't have happened. If Dad hadn't been so useless, she wouldn't even have gone. Even then, as I was sitting up in bed, I blamed Dad. I tried not to, but I couldn't help myself. I knew that I was cross all the time because of the muddle I was feeling. Ella's quietness was to do with the muddle she was feeling too. Jude was getting very babyish, even though she thought she was so grown-up for six. She'd suck her thumb and want bedtime stories that were meant for four-year-olds, and sometimes she'd even wet the bed, which drove Dad demented because of all the washing and having to go to the launderette. So maybe Jude was miserable as well.

Down the hall, Dad's shrill alarm went off. It was eight o'clock then. I was sorry because I needed more thinking time, and in a minute Dad would be in to rouse me and he'd wake Ella and Jude and the day would start with all its noise and bustle and

21

there wouldn't be any space for private thoughts. Only Mum had known how much I thought about things. Everybody else thought it was only Ella who worried about what was going on. But Mum had understood that I had lots of ideas and feelings that I kept inside myself because it was easier than having to explain them. Besides, nobody understood. Ella was important because she was the oldest. Jude was important because she was the baby. But when you were stuck in the middle, you were practically nobody and you were just ignored unless you made a lot of noise. Sometimes, though, I got fed up with being loud and fighting for people's attention all the time. That was why I liked being in bed, though I never let on. In bed, I could do whatever I wanted, and nobody even knew.

'Bessie! It's time you were up.' Dad was in and out faster than Concorde. It had started then – the new day. I sighed and went to the others' room to see what they were up to. Jude forgot she was on the bottom bunk and tried to stand up in bed. Her hair got tangled up in the rough wooden slats above. 'Hold still,' I said, going over to her, 'you're making it worse.'

'It's all tangled!'

'I know it is. I'm trying to get you out.'

We each have the same curly African hair, but Jude's was quite long, it was past her shoulders. 'You've got your Dad's hair,' Mum would say to her. 'We're a family of many different nations.' It was true. The African–Caribbean part came from Mum and there was Scottish and Canadian ancestry on my father's side. I was supposed to look like Dad's father, according to Mum, but like all our relatives on Dad's side he'd died before we were born, so I didn't know for sure. My skin's mid-brown like my sisters' but there's something special about me. My eyes are brownish-green. It's one of the first things people notice. Witch's eyes, Mum used to say, and she'd call me her little witch, and I'd liked that, it had made me feel different, not like anybody else. Special. I twisted Jude's hair round my fingers. It needed some moisturizer and a good, comb-in conditioner. So did mine, come to think of it. Mum had always bought those things for us. Even though Dad had once worked for a company that made toiletries, it never seemed to occur to him that our type of hair needed special treatment in order to shine and look healthy. There were so many things he should have been sorting out for us, but nothing seemed to happen. I gave Jude's hair one last tug and she was free.

'I want to sleep on the top bunk,' she wailed.

'Well you can't, it's mine,' said Ella, sitting up.

'Go on. Please.'

Usually when people begged for anything Ella found it hard to refuse them. That was how I'd got my room. I waited for Ella to tell Jude she could have the top bunk after all, but she kept on saying no, even when Jude started whimpering. I was impressed. Maybe Ella was getting harder in her old age. It would make arguments less predictable and a lot more fun if Ella livened up a bit. I was getting cold, so I went back to my room and dragged the box labelled BESSIE'S CLOTHES from under the bed. My favourite shirt was missing. Ella probably had it. I grabbed an old blue one that I hadn't worn in weeks. I knew that if I didn't hurry up, I'd be last in the queue for the bathroom.

It was just as I'd feared. Ella had got there first when no one was looking.

'I was ahead of you,' I said as the door was closing. 'I've been awake for hours.'

'Awake doesn't count. Only up counts.'

I wondered if it was worth a full-scale fight and decided that it wasn't. I could beat Ella into submission any time I liked, but why fight when you're not even sure you want to be up in the first place? I went back to bed, snuggling under the blankets.

I was awoken by Dad's shouts. 'If you're not down this minute, I'll be up there to pull the covers off. Or I'll send Jude!'

Threatening me with Jude was a smart move. She seemed so small and cute but she was capable of all kinds of tortures when you were only half awake and couldn't defend yourself. It was better to get up.

I put a sweatshirt on over my pyjamas. My arms were too long so the sleeves stopped an inch above my wrists. Sometimes I wished I wasn't so tall. I was taller than Ella, even though she was thirteen and a half. Everybody thought I was the oldest and often ignored Ella when we were out. What would your little sisters like? they'd ask me, ham sandwiches or cheese? Of course, I never enlightened

24

them, I enjoyed pretending to be the oldest too much for that. They don't like cheese, I would reply, but it wasn't true, it was just that I preferred ham.

I stubbed my toe on my way to the kitchen. 'Hell!' I said. It was the only swear word we were allowed. I hobbled downstairs, but nobody took any notice. They were busy scraping burnt bits off the toast.

'You should have saved them for me. You know I like toast burnt.'

'You're weird,' said Jude.

I took it as a compliment.

'What will you all do today?' asked Dad, as if we were spoilt for choice.

'Don't know,' I said. 'When are we getting a telly?'

'Soon. I have to get in touch with the rental people.'

'Are we going to have a video recorder like we did in the old house?'

'Can't you think of anything except what you want?'

Dad sounded as if he was going to lose his temper, so Ella said quickly, 'I thought I'd go exploring. I want to see what it's like here.'

'No,' said Dad.

Ella fell silent, so I said, 'Come on Dad, what do you mean, no?'

'Just what I say. You're in London now, it's different here. You've got to be careful.'

'I'm thirteen,' said Ella hopefully.

'Makes no difference. I don't want you out on your own.'

'But Dad, it's crazy,' I said. 'No one of our age stays in all the time.'

'They do now.'

'In three years' time, I'll be old enough to get married,' said Ella.

But Dad wasn't having any. 'No, you two, I mean it. I want you here, where I know it's safe.'

'We couldn't be safe in this crummy old house. The roof will probably fall on top of us. What's safe about that?'

'Change the record, Bessie,' said Dad.

I felt like crying. How was I going to like living in London if Dad wouldn't even let me out of the house? I couldn't imagine what it would be like to stay indoors all the time. It would be impossible, a nightmare.

'Go and get dressed, Bessie,' Dad said. 'You should have sorted yourself out hours ago.'

'If I can't go out, there's no point in dressing, is there?'

'Just do it, Bess.'

'Oh, all right!' I banged up the stairs, making as much noise as I could, though that particular protest gesture was starting to bore even me. It was hard though, to think of other forms of expression that wouldn't put Dad in an even worse mood. I went into the bathroom and filled the basin with hot water. Jude must have used it after Ella because there was a dirt ring round the plug hole. The kid never cleaned up after herself and Dad never made her. It wasn't fair.

Downstairs, Dad was yelling at Ella. I didn't know what she'd done, but it sounded as if she'd spilt something because Dad was telling her to clean up all the mess. I didn't often feel sorry for Ella, but I thought it was mean of him to shout. She was sobbing loudly, I could hear it. Ella wasn't like me and Jude, she tried so hard to be good. Why couldn't he see that she would only do something wrong if she really couldn't help it?

Jude had used up most of the soap. There was just a thin sliver left. Such a clean girl, I thought sarcastically, she gets through at least a bar of soap a day. I knelt down and opened the cupboard under the washstand. It was packed with the Feel Good range. I looked at it in surprise. It hadn't occurred to me that Dad had brought any of it with us. It was part of the old life, wasn't it? It didn't belong here.

I opened a bottle of Feel Good Shampoo for Fair Hair. Dad was the only fair-haired person in our house, but I knew he never used it. He didn't like the scent, but of course he never let on at work. I remembered the very first time Dad had brought Feel Good home. He'd just been made assistant manager at the factory where it was produced. We'd all been so excited. Mum had said we ought to celebrate, so we'd drunk to Feel Good with fizzy lemonade. Someone else was doing Dad's job now. The factory owners said they were sorry about Mum's death, but they couldn't wait for him to get over it any longer, they had a business to run. So now there was very little money coming into the house.

I pulled the plug out of the basin and watched the water gurgle down the hole. Then I poured a whole bottle of Feel Good Shampoo down the sink, and followed it with Feel Good Conditioner. I enjoyed the wastefulness. I was sick of being careful all the time. It was as if I was pouring away a useless piece of the past.

Jude was banging on the door. There was something wrong with the kid, I was sure of it. She never stopped needing to go to the toilet.

'What's that smell?' she said as I let her in.

'What smell?' I asked innocently.

'Feel Good.'

'No, I don't, not very.'

'Don't be silly,' said Jude, giggling. 'I meant it smelt like Feel Good in here.'

'There isn't any Feel Good,' I told her crossly. I dropped the empty bottles into the bin.

Three

'If you're going to make that much noise you can go into the yard and do it!'

I gave Dad my meanest look. We weren't making a lot of noise, and we had to do something to keep us occupied now that we didn't even have a telly. 'We can't play outside,' I said crossly. 'In case you haven't noticed, it's pouring with rain.'

Dad looked startled, and it was obvious that he hadn't noticed. I wondered how he'd manage if we weren't there to point everything out to him.

We were playing a really good game of hide-and-seek. It had been my idea. The house was small, but it had some spooky dark corners, and if you didn't turn on any lights it was all shadows and creepy bits, perfect for making yourself almost invisible and scaring yourself half to death at the same time. If you couldn't shriek when you were searching for your sisters' mouldering bodies in the ruins, there really wasn't much point in continuing the game.

'We'll try to be quiet, Dad,' said Ella.

'We can't be quiet, it'll spoil the game,' I said. 'We wouldn't have to make so much noise if we had a telly to watch. You said you'd get one for us.'

Dad sighed. 'They want a deposit. I can't give them one before next week.'

'Well, what are we supposed to do?'

Dad banged his fist on the kitchen table. 'Whatever you like, but stop bothering me, all right?'

Ella and Jude both apologized meekly but I continued to glare. Ella nudged me meaningfully, so I said, 'But I'm not sorry,' under my breath.

'Just say it,' replied Ella in a loud whisper.

'No!' I was tired of being made to feel bad all the time for doing ordinary things. It wasn't fair.

Dad said, 'I'm getting fed up with you, Bess.'

'Not half as fed up as I am with you!' I yelled.

Dad stood up suddenly and I was scared. 'Go upstairs, all of you!' he shouted.

'No!' I shouted back.

'Come on,' said Ella, grabbing my hand.

I wrenched myself free and ran towards the door, closely followed by Jude. I slammed the door behind me, and as it banged shut, Jude's fingers were trapped. There was a moment of silence and then she started to scream. I stood still in the doorway, just looking at her. I hadn't meant to do it, it was an accident. 'I'm sorry,' I said softly, but nobody heard. Ella was holding Jude and Dad had gone to get a wet cloth. He came back and wrapped it around Jude's fingers. Her screams had become sobs and she was trembling. I ran upstairs.

Suddenly, everything was like a dream. I was so scared of what I'd done that I couldn't see straight. No one would ever forgive me, I knew they wouldn't. I went over to the window. In the yard opposite, there was a boy of about Ella's age, playing with a fierce-looking dog, even though the rain was coming down in torrents. I wished I was out there with them. Why had I argued with Dad? If only I'd kept my mouth shut, none of it would have happened.

Ella came in. 'What's happening?' I said curtly, not taking my eyes off the boy in the opposite yard.

'We're going to the hospital.'

My stomach flipped over. 'Why?' I said, as coolly as I could.

'Dad thinks one of Jude's fingers might be broken.'

I began to cry silently, but I just kept staring at the boy with the dog.

'It was an accident,' said Ella, coming up behind me. 'You didn't mean to do it, I know that. It's OK, Bess, don't cry.'

The fact that Ella was being so nice made me feel worse. I started to cry even more then, heaving, hiccupping crying.

'Jude knows you didn't mean it. Even Dad knows,' said Ella. 'Come on, get your jacket. Dad wants to take her there as fast as he can.'

The red double-decker bus took ages to get to the hospital. It inched along streets that were too narrow and heaved out fumes impatiently at traffic lights. Jude was sitting beside Dad, who was staring out of the window. Every now and then he patted her absently and said, 'Nearly there now.'

I looked at Ella. 'Doesn't he know where the

31

hospital is? He's been saying that for the last half hour.'

'It's not far, it's just that the bus is slow,' said Ella. 'Here, have this,' she said, pushing something into my hand. It was a lollypop, the sort of thing you use to shut up a two-year-old. I looked towards Jude. 'What about her?' I said. It didn't seem fair that I should have a treat when she was the one who'd got hurt.

'I offered it to her first. She didn't want it.'

I wasn't sure I could stomach one of Jude's rejects, but it seemed ungrateful to say so in the circumstances. I unwrapped the lolly and stuck it in my mouth. I knew then why Ella had been so keen for me to have it. It was so big that it would be at least five minutes before I'd be able to speak again.

A large, grey building loomed ahead. We got off the bus at the entrance and filed inside, not talking. Hospitals are like libraries or churches; you have to behave well and only speak in whispers.

'Where are we going?' asked Jude, in a panicky voice.

'Accident and Emergency,' answered Dad.

'Am I an emergency?' said Jude, perking up a bit.

'No, you're an accident.'

'But it wasn't an accident,' Jude replied.

'It was!' I said sharply, and two elderly women turned to stare.

'Be quiet, both of you,' said Dad. 'Bessie didn't do it on purpose, Jude.'

I was touched that he was sticking up for me in spite of the argument we'd had. Sometimes it was as if he didn't know, or care, that we existed, but at other times he was a proper dad, the kind I'd always wanted to have.

The Accident and Emergency department was packed. People with bandaged arms or heads lolled on plastic seats, half asleep. I couldn't help staring. It was easy to work out what was wrong with the bandaged ones, but there were lots of others with no obvious injuries. 'What's the matter with him?' I asked Ella, pointing to a youngish man who was leaning, bored, against the wall.

Ella shrugged. 'Maybe he's waiting for someone who's hurt.'

Like us, I thought, and I wished more than anything that I hadn't slammed that door.

The waiting seemed endless. I began to drum lightly on the seat in front of me. 'Don't, Bess,' said Dad in strained tones. 'It's irritating.'

I subsided and stuffed my fingers into my pockets. I didn't know what to do with myself. 'Can I go over there?' I said eventually, looking towards the large double entrance.

'What for?' said Dad.

I shrugged and stayed where I was.

'How much longer?' wailed Jude. 'My fingers hurt.'

'Not long now,' said Dad, though I knew he was no wiser than we were.

Jude wasn't convinced either. 'You keep saying that, but it's been ages.'

'Shut up,' Dad said. Then he seemed to remember that Jude had been hurt and he added in kinder tones, 'It won't be much longer, you'll see.'

But it was another hour and a half before Jude was seen by a woman in a white coat with a stethoscope around her neck.

'Aren't you going to use that on me?' asked Jude, once her fingers had been examined.

'It's for chests,' said the doctor, 'and your chest looks fine to me.'

Jude looked disappointed.

'But I am going to send you up to X-ray, and when you get back, I'm going to get the nurse to give you a big, white bandage.'

Jude was enchanted. 'A really big one that everyone can see?'

'I wouldn't be surprised,' said the doctor.

'Little exhibitionist,' I muttered. It was one of Mum's phrases, and she used to say it to me all the time, but not in a nasty way. When she'd said it, it had sounded kind and funny and it had made me feel good.

Then the doctor asked how the accident had happened, so I left the cubicle and stood outside.

There was a yellow stripe painted up the corridor. You had to go along it to find out where the X-ray department was. 'Follow the yellow brick road,' Ella joked as they all came out. Then she added, 'Dad, I'm a bit thirsty.'

We all knew that if Ella was asking for something, however indirectly, she had to be absolutely desperate. Dad spoke kindly to her. 'Sorry, love, you'll have to hold on until we're out of here.'

I said, 'There's a cafeteria. I saw a sign back there.'

Dad looked at his watch. 'I suppose it has been a long afternoon. All right, you can both go. Get something for yourselves and a drink for Jude. I'll meet you up there when we're through.' He pushed a coin into Ella's hand.

'But that's only a pound,' I said. 'You won't get three drinks for that.'

'Then share, and think yourselves lucky because that's all I've got,' said Dad crossly.

Ella and I wandered up the staircase, past the children's ward. I was glad they weren't keeping Jude in.

As we paused to look at the *Alice in Wonderland* posters on the walls, Ella said, 'I wish you wouldn't argue about everything. We're only here because you argued.'

I started walking quickly again. It was obvious that Ella hadn't really forgiven me, she'd only been pretending. Dad probably hadn't either. I felt tears welling, but I was determined not to cry. What was it Mum used to say? *It's no good crying over spilt milk.* It's true. Once something's done, that's that, and you just have to get on and forget it.

The cafeteria was for patients and visitors and it was painted yellow, pink and white, like an over-iced birthday cake. I picked up a tray and selected a carton of apple juice. 'No, get orange squash,' said Ella. 'It's cheaper.' We paid for the drinks and went to sit at a corner table by the window.

It was boring, just sitting, counting the minutes. I pulled off my shoe and curled my toes around the table leg. It was then that I caught sight of a woman coming towards us. I thought it was Mum. For a moment, all the months since her death were wiped out and I pushed my chair back and began to run towards her. It was only as I reached her that I realized she was older, her brown face was wrinkled and there were streaks of grey in her blue-black hair. I stopped, full of confusion, and she said 'Bessie' to me, so kindly and gently, just the way Mum always did.

'Gran,' I said, and I put my arms around her and hugged her tight.

She hugged me back, and then Ella came and we were all hugging, and I was crying a bit, though I pretended that I wasn't.

We went to sit down again. She bought us each doughnuts with real dairy cream and cans of ginger beer.

'Where's Jude and your father?' asked Gran as we started eating.

'In X-ray,' Ella explained. 'Jude shut her fingers in a door. That's why we're here.'

I fingered my paper cup, embarrassed, half expecting Ella to give her chapter and verse concerning the accident, but she didn't say anything more.

'You haven't written,' I said after a pause. It sounded accusing, but I couldn't help it.

'I don't have your new address,' Gran replied.

Ella said, 'Hasn't Dad —?'

Gran shook her head. 'It's a bad time for your father, I know that.'

'But he should have told you where we were, we wanted to see you,' I said. 'I'm fed up with him, he's so –'

'Hush, Bess. You don't speak about your father like that.'

'I wish he wasn't my dad, I hate him, I –'

Ella nudged me hard. Dad was coming towards us. His stride was angry. He was pulling Jude by her good hand and she was looking scared. He reached the table.

'Hello, Stephen,' said Gran.

Dad didn't return the greeting. 'What are you doing here?' was all he said.

'Arthritis. I come here for physiotherapy once a fortnight. How are you, Steve?'

'We're fine. Come on,' he added, letting go of Jude and taking me by the arm instead. 'We're going home.'

'What about my drink?' Jude said.

'We're going home,' Dad repeated, no longer looking at Gran.

'But Dad –' said Jude and me together.

Gran said, 'Stephen, please, let me talk to you for a minute. It must be hard for you without Lou, and the children, they miss their mother. Life's too short for bad feeling. We all said things we didn't mean, it was the shock of Lou's death, I don't blame you, of course I don't, I was wrong and I'm sorry.'

'It's too late,' said Dad.

'Don't say that. Couldn't you all stay a while?

It's been so many months. Now you're in London, I could see more of the children. It would mean a lot to me.'

'No,' said Dad. He began to walk towards the door. Ella, Jude and me followed behind, embarrassed, not sure what to think. Gran followed too.

'For Lou's sake, Stephen. She wouldn't want all of this sadness. We need each other more than ever now.'

'No, I don't want you interfering, I'll bring up the children my way. There were enough accusations at the funeral. I'm not having all that starting up again now.'

'No accusations, no interference, I promise,' said Gran.

'Come on, kids,' said Dad. 'We're going home.'

'At least give me your address. Please.'

'We're going home,' repeated Dad.

'Gran,' said Jude, reaching for her hand. Dad pulled her back.

'Aren't you even going to let us speak to Gran?' I said.

Dad ignored me. He kept on walking.

'You can't stop us seeing her, it isn't fair,' I said.

Dad said, 'She'd take you all away from me if she could. I'm going to see that she doesn't.'

'No, Stephen, I never meant –' said Gran.

He walked away, leaving her sentence hanging in the air.

Jude was crying now. 'I want Gran,' she sobbed, and then she added breathlessly, 'and I want Mummy too.'

'Do you think I don't?' said Dad, with sadness in his voice.

I looked back. Gran was behind us, following, I thought. I held her gaze, hoping that she would come after us, and take us home to live with her, but then she stopped. She just stood there, watching silently, until we were out of sight.

Four

I hadn't realized how much I'd taken the television for granted when we'd lived in the old house. Now we were gathered round the empty space where it ought to have been standing. I was doing a jigsaw puzzle. Dad was just sitting there. Ella had a book in front of her, but she wasn't reading it. Jude was stroking the toy cat on her knee, pretending it was real.

We'd had a proper cat at the old house. He was a tortoiseshell called Jim, only Jim hadn't been a male cat at all, we'd discovered that when we'd taken it to the vet. Eventually there had been kittens, six of them, and homes to be found for them all. They'd been so cute, small and fubsy with little pink mouths and screwed-up eyes. Jim had been a good mother, patient and loving. I wondered what she was doing now. She usually sat on the garden wall at this time of day, cleaning herself or just gazing at the world. Now the people who used to be our next-door neighbours were feeding her and caring for her. I hoped she was OK and that she wasn't missing us. That wasn't quite true. I hoped Jim *was* missing us because it would prove that she still loved us and that we mattered to her.

My thoughts turned again to Gran. I'd been

wanting to ask why we weren't allowed to see her ever since we'd come home, but something in Dad's manner was telling me not to. He was staring at the wall in front of him, not looking at any of us. We might as well have been in another room, another planet, another universe, for all the notice he took of us. I hated it when Dad was like this. He'd been like it just after Mum had died. It had been as if we no longer existed.

Gran had said she was sorry. Sorry for what? I wanted to know. I was tired of sitting in front of a television that didn't exist pretending that our lives hadn't changed.

'Dad, can I go down in the cellar? I want to do some more unpacking.' He didn't answer me. I waited for a few moments and then I repeated the question, but he still didn't speak. I went over and stood by his chair. I nudged him. 'Dad?' I said.

'What is it?' he asked.

'Can I do some more unpacking?' I said as patiently as I could.

'If you want to,' he said, and he went back to gazing at the wall. Still, at least he hadn't guessed what I wanted to do.

Ella was looking at me quizzically. It was a look which said, since when have you been interested in unpacking boxes? I decided to make a quick exit. For all her quietness, Ella wasn't exactly stupid.

We'd been using the cellar for hide-and-seek yesterday. It was rather like a dungeon. The plaster walls were peeling and there were green damp patches on the stone floor. Water dripped steadily from an unknown source. I saw my breath and realized how cold it was down there. I'd have to be careful not to get pneumonia. I dragged some of the boxes out of the far corner. Ella had labelled them, which was lucky because I figured that somewhere there ought to be at least one that said PHOTO ALBUMS. It took me some minutes to find it. I paused for a while, just staring at the cardboard, not sure what I was going to discover. I opened the box slowly and took out the oldest-looking album. I began to turn the pages.

At once, I knew that the photo album was a bad idea. There were pictures of my mother in it. Tears came suddenly and I smeared them out of my eyes with my fingertips. Get a grip, Bess, I said to myself. I continued to turn the pages. There was Gran, looking thinner than she does now, and with thicker, longer hair. She did look like Mum. I knew I hadn't imagined it. I hadn't really been aware of that before. I suppose that sounds funny, but before Mum died, she'd just been Gran, I hadn't thought about family resemblances, who I took after and how I fitted into things, I'd just taken it for granted. And now Mum was gone and nothing could be taken for granted any more.

So why was Dad keeping us away from Gran? Why wouldn't he even speak to her properly? Had they quarrelled? What about? I wanted to know. It wasn't only curiosity now, it was something far more urgent than that. My heart was beating so fast I was afraid I was going to have a heart attack. I sat still for a moment, trying to calm myself. I only half knew why I was so scared but it was to do with feeling alone. Mum had gone, and Dad was letting Gran go too. I'd belonged to them, with them, and now suddenly I didn't have any real belonging any more. I shut the photo album and went back upstairs.

They were all still sitting just as I'd left them, like when you push the pause button on a video recorder. 'Dad,' I said, but as usual, he didn't respond first time. I crouched beside his chair. 'Dad, why can't we see Gran any more? What did she do?'

Ella looked alarmed. She signalled to me to shut up, but I was determined to ignore her.

'Why didn't you let Gran speak to you yesterday?' I demanded.

'It's time to put the dinner on,' said Dad, as if I was invisible.

'I'm not hungry,' I said, though it wasn't true. I'm always hungry.

'I'm hungry,' said Jude. I glared at her.

'Go on, Ella, and you too, Bessie. Go and make a start on the vegetables. I'll come and see to the rest of it later.'

'Was there a quarrel? Just tell me that.'

There was a long silence. Then Dad said, 'Your grandmother thought it was my fault, the accident, I mean. She said I wouldn't be able to look after you adequately. Does that answer your question?'

'At the hospital, she said she was sorry, and she hadn't meant the things she said.'

43

'I'm not telling you again Bess, go with Ella and put the dinner on.'

I opened my mouth to argue, but closed it again. Dad was looking angry. I followed Ella into the kitchen. We shut the door behind us.

Ella leant against it wearily and said, 'What did you do that for? He said yesterday that he didn't want to talk about it. Why did you have to go poking around? If he gets really depressed, what'll we do? Mum's not here, it'll be up to me. It's all right for you, you don't have to deal with everything the way I do. You're not the oldest, it's not up to you to cope.' Ella was almost crying. It made me feel bad, which then made me cross.

'I don't see why we have to be good and nice all the time just to stop him being ill. It isn't fair. Why can't we just be normal?'

Ella got the potato peeler out of the drawer and tipped some potatoes into the sink. 'There are carrots in the cupboard, Bess,' she said.

'Don't you want to know what's going on, Ella?'

'No, not especially.'

'Go on, you must.'

'No. Bess, I'm scared of what he'll do. Remember all those times . . . ?'

I did remember. Once, long before Mum's accident, he'd locked himself in his room and refused to come out and he hadn't spoken to anyone for days and days. The doctor had come and he'd been taken to hospital. He'd stayed there for weeks. Another time, he'd had a row with a neighbour about their dog and he'd just gone off without telling anyone, even Mum, and he'd been gone for ages. Then he'd turned up again as if nothing had happened and he didn't seem to remember the row or even that he'd been away.

Ella took out the potato peelings and poured the muddy water into the sink. She got out some fish fingers. 'I don't want him to get depressed again, Bess, not really bad. You do understand, don't you?'

In a way, I did understand, but it also made me angry. Dad's moods meant that you could never say how you really felt about anything without him going funny about it. It meant that whatever happened, he was the most important person in the house. We had to think about what he wanted all the time. He ruled everything just by being depressed. I decided that when I grew up, I'd be very depressed indeed, and no one would be allowed to upset me at all, not ever. I said to Ella, 'I'm pretty depressed you know,' but Ella only laughed at me and went to light the grill.

That evening, after we'd eaten, I decided that if Dad wasn't going to let us see Gran, he could at least let us go out somewhere that would take our minds off the situation. I went up to my room, the only place where I could think private thoughts uninterrupted.

I got the train set running and settled down to watch its steady movement. Ella was getting bossy, I decided. She seemed to think that the running of the house was up to her, and it wasn't. Dad confided in Ella, and he babied Jude, but I might as well have disappeared completely. Nobody was interested in what was happening to me. If I went down to breakfast stark naked with a banana stuffed in each ear, no one would even notice. The thought had a certain appeal. I wondered if I should arrange it, but then I remembered that we couldn't afford bananas any more; the odd apple was all we got nowadays.

It was so dull being here in London, and it didn't need to be. I'd read all about the parks and shops and museums but we'd scarcely been to one. There were red buses to be ridden round the city and underground trains to be explored and the Docklands Light Railway and . . . thinking about it made me cross. Dad was daft not to let us go anywhere, we'd been allowed to go to loads of places back in Leeds.

I got a piece of paper out of the cupboard and began to draw the Tower of London. I'd seen a picture of it in a book and I was trying to remember all the details. I was glad I had my own room and didn't have to share with Jude. When you shared, half your things got borrowed without people even asking. It was useless, living with your family. Even as I thought it, I realized I wasn't living with my family any more, or at least, not with all my family, not with Mum.

I drew an outline of a raven, or that was what it was meant to be, but I couldn't remember exactly what ravens looked like, so it resembled a pigeon more than anything. I'd seen lots of pigeons in

London, and they made a heck of a mess, their droppings were everywhere. Thinking about pigeons reminded me of how much I hated spiders, so I did a quick search of my room as I always did when I thought of creeping spider legs. I opened all the cupboards and checked under the bed. It took about five minutes, and even then I wasn't quite satisfied. One might have been hiding in a little corner somewhere. It was probably laughing its legs off to think I hadn't spotted it.

I went to get another sheet of paper from the cupboard and noticed an orange bit of paper sticking out from under a book. It was the notice about the youth club. If only Ella and I could go and find something to do in this dump, I thought. I went downstairs and asked Dad if he'd let us.

There was a long pause and then he said slowly, 'What youth club is this?'

I sighed. I hated slow-motion conversations. I wanted to crank Dad up. I explained, adding that I thought it was run by a church. I thought Dad might go for that – churches seemed safe and respectable. Then real inspiration struck, and I said, 'If you let me, I'll be really good. I'll help around the house without complaining, and . . .' I paused here. I didn't want to be too obvious about anything '. . . and I won't talk about anything you don't want me to talk about.'

I gave Dad a sideways glance. This form of persuasion seemed to be working. Dad looked more interested than he'd been before – not that this was saying much. Then he said, 'Go away, Bessie. Let me talk to Ella about it.'

'Why? I'm telling you about it, you don't need Ella to tell you.'

'Bessie, let me talk to Ella, OK? I'm not agreeing to anything until I've talked to her.'

'Oh, all right.' I stomped out of the room and went into the kitchen. Ella was clearing up the remains of the meal, which made me feel slightly guilty; I should have been helping. I explained why Dad wanted her and added, 'I think he'll agree to let us go if you tell him it's near, and I've said it's for elevens to fourteens.'

'That's a lie. It's for twelve years up,' said Ella self-righteously.

'It's not really a lie. No one will know. I look old enough. Anyway, you wouldn't want to go on your own, would you?'

'I wouldn't mind,' said Ella, and I thought, look who's lying now. Then she said, 'I hope you haven't upset him again.'

'He's going to be upset sometimes, that's life. We can't just do everything we're supposed to all the time in case he gets moody about it.'

'Kids do what their parents tell them to. That's life as well.'

'I know,' I said impatiently, 'but this is different. He wouldn't mind us going out if Mum was still here.' I wanted to say more, but I wasn't sure how to put it. I just knew that the reins had got a lot tighter since Mum's accident, and that when Dad was in one of his moods, he wasn't always fair and he wasn't always right.

Ella dried her hands on the tea towel and handed me the dishcloth. 'If I've got to go and talk to Dad about this youth club and lie so that you can come too, you'd better start doing your share of the housework.'

I almost liked Ella then. That's just what I would have said if the roles had been reversed.

Five

I suppose it wasn't much, being allowed to go to the youth club, but I felt happy for the first time in weeks. At last, Ella and I were out on our own, seeing something of London and not being nagged by Dad. It was good to get away from him and out of the house. All that gloom and despondency was catching. I skipped along the pavement and then remembered I was trying to pass for twelve, so I matched Ella's strides and tried to look grown-up.

I could see that Ella wasn't as happy as I was. She was walking with her head down and her fists clenched tightly at her side. Then suddenly she said, 'Bessie, do you think Dad really is looking for work? I mean, have you seen him with the papers, posting letters or anything like that?'

I shook my head, and some of the happiness that being out had brought began to fade.

'I wonder how much money we've got?'

I shrugged. That was grown-up stuff, it wasn't for us to worry about. Dad would sort it out. He had to.

'There are things he should be doing,' Ella continued. 'When you're out of work, you have to sign on or you don't get any money. Dad hasn't been out of the house except to get food.'

'Maybe he's off sick,' I said.

'But you have to go to the doctor. He hasn't been, I'm sure he hasn't . . . And then there's school. We're supposed to go, it's the law. Dad hasn't even mentioned it. Has he mentioned it to you?'

I shook my head and wished Ella would shut up about all this stuff. I knew that she was fretting about leaving Dad on his own. She couldn't even go out for an evening without getting into a state. It was as if she was the grown-up and Dad was the kid.

I walked on ahead to stop her talking to me about Dad and spoiling my good mood. I was fed up with her worrying. She'd been getting on to me all week about winding Dad up, as if I was doing it on purpose. She didn't seem to understand that Dad and I were programmed to clash and there wasn't much that we could do about it. Ella was like him in a lot of ways. She was shy with people and didn't like going out much and she worried all the time. I mean, I worry more than people think, but I know when to stop, I don't worry about what can't be helped. Dad and Ella worried about absolutely everything, even things that hadn't happened yet. Fancy worrying that Dad hadn't sorted out a school for us. I mean, that is perverse. The longer it took Dad the better, as far as I was concerned.

It was just before six in the evening and the streets were full of people coming home from work. In spite of the distance I was putting between us, Ella's comments had got to me and I couldn't help thinking about how it used to be for us when Mum and

Dad had both had jobs. This had been my favourite time of day. Mum and us kids used to get in at about four and then Dad would come home an hour or two later. We'd eat about now. I could almost smell the meat and potatoes, but it wasn't just the food, it was a sense of the rightness of things. I suppose that sounds strange, and I don't know how to explain it better. Mum used to have a saying: 'All's right with the world.' It meant there was a kind of safety about everything and that was how it had been with Mum and Dad at home in Leeds. Sure, Dad had still had moods. Sometimes he and Mum had quarrelled about them. I remembered then that one such quarrel had occurred on the day of the accident and it had made Mum drive off in that car. It halted my thoughts for a moment and I felt panic welling up in me. I put the memory aside and replaced it with the smaller problems we had had in our old life back in Leeds. There was the way I was always being told off for leaving my room in a mess and the fact that Ella and I had argued most of the time. Jude had been as irritating as ever then, and of course there had been chores to get done and rows about whether Mum was going to let me have red shoes (which I couldn't wear to school) or brown ones which were practical but hideous. But nearly all of these had been every-day problems, they'd kept us all feeling and think-ing and breathing, there was nothing scary about them. I suppose, in a way, they were reassuring, because they were predictable. I always knew what would happen if I left my clothes on the floor or if

I bashed Jude for 'borrowing' my stuff; there were no nasty surprises. I never imagined then, in those safe Leeds days, that I would ever miss such things. Now, here in London, I would have given anything to have them back again.

Ella caught up with me. She said, 'You know, Bess, I really wish you hadn't stirred up all that stuff about Gran. It made Dad a lot worse. If Dad doesn't want us to keep in touch with her, he has a good reason and we should just leave it.'

'Shut up,' I said.

'Do you know what'll happen if Dad stops being able to take care of us? The social will be round. They could put us into care.'

'I said shut up!' I answered angrily. How could Ella not mind the possibility that we would never see our gran again? Why could she never see that Dad could be wrong and we could be right?

The hall seemed much further than I'd thought. We went on in silence until we reached the entrance. It was brightly lit, and we could hear a set of drums being played. We stood by the door for a moment. Although I wouldn't have admitted it to Ella, I felt a bit awkward. It was all so unfamiliar. We edged our way inside.

A man came up to us straight away and said his name was Mike. He asked us what we were called and where we lived and then offered to introduce us to some of the regulars. As he led us across the room, Ella said, 'At least he didn't ask how old we are.'

'It doesn't matter about you,' I replied scornfully, 'so what are you worried about?'

A boy and a girl were playing snooker in the corner of the room. The girl was the same height as me and the boy was a little taller, but they were both stocky. I watched them play for a moment. The boy didn't miss a shot, and he studied the ball with professional intensity. The girl waited her turn patiently. She leant on her cue, chewing gum and wearing a baseball cap. They looked like brother and sister. They each had dark brown skin and their hair was curly and short. Something about them reminded me of Mum. It was the best and the worst feeling at exactly the same time.

Mike said, 'Shirley, Carl, meet Ella and Bess.'

They nodded coolly in our direction but they remained silent. Shirley took over at the snooker table and potted a ball with a flourish of her cue. I memorized the movement, determined to try it later.

It was awkward, just standing there so I picked up a cue and tried to look as if I knew how to use it. Shirley nudged me out of the way and took a shot at the blue ball. She whammed it into the pocket.

'Can I have a go?' I said. I just wanted them to notice I existed.

'We were here first,' said Carl.

'When you've finished then.'

They didn't answer.

I sat on a nearby stool, glad for once that Ella was there too. At least they were ignoring both of us, not just me. It took them about twenty minutes to finish their game. Each shot was studied with care before it was taken. In that twenty minutes, I learnt more about the game than I would have thought possible. They were artists.

At last the game was over. They gestured to me to come over to the table. I picked up the cue. I so much wanted to impress them. I lined up the balls and aimed carefully as they had done. I took the shot. The cue just clipped the side of the ball. It trickled a little way down the green baize before coming to a stop.

'Can't you play?' asked Shirley mildly.

I wanted to claim that I'd been unlucky, that I was the best snooker player in the business, but I knew they wouldn't be fooled. 'No,' was all I said.

Shirley suddenly grinned and said, 'At least you're honest,' and I was glad I'd told the truth for once. It was funny how much I wanted to please her, even though we'd only just met. I don't usually like people straight away, I test them out a bit first and see if I can be bothered with them. Most people are pretty pathetic, they let you down, so it's best to wait and see. With Shirley though, it was different, or perhaps it was just that I was feeling a bit lonely without Dawn and Sally, my friends in Leeds. Whatever it was, when she said, 'I'll teach you to play if you like,' I was as pleased as I could be, though I certainly didn't show it. I've got more cool than that.

She was a good teacher; she had me hitting those balls straight in no time. And she was patient too, she didn't yell when I did something stupid. Once or twice I glanced towards Ella and saw that Carl had taken her under his wing and was chatting to her at a corner table. They were both drinking Cokes with ice and a slice of lemon. Ella looked relaxed. Usually, when she talks to someone, she looks edgy, she fidgets a lot and doesn't look them in the eye, so I was glad she was OK – I reckoned it might keep her off my back for a while if she had someone other than family to think about. I potted the last ball into the pocket, the way that Shirley had shown me, and decided I needed a drink too. I counted out the money Dad had given me and wished there'd been more – I didn't want to look like one of the world's poor in front of Shirley. But the funny thing was, she was counting out her money too, and saying she didn't have enough for a large Coke, just a small one, so we had something in common there too. We joined Ella and Carl, who were already behaving like best pals.

'How old are you?' asked Carl suddenly, looking at Ella.

'Thirteen,' Ella replied.

'I'm thirteen too. How old's your sister?'

'She's –' I knew Ella had been about to say eleven, but she'd stopped herself just in time. Instead, she said, 'She's fourteen,' and I realized things couldn't have worked out better for me. Everyone would think I was the eldest now, and they'd ask me things and treat me with respect.

'She doesn't look fourteen, but then you don't look your age either. Is everyone small in your family?' It was then that I realized that Carl had no tact whatsoever.

'I suppose we are quite small,' said Ella, though it wasn't true. Dad's tall, he's almost six foot, though Mum was only five feet two. 'How old are you, Shirley?' Ella asked.

Shirley and Carl exchanged glances. Then Carl leant forward and said, 'Can we trust you?'

Ella and I nodded gravely. We're not the betraying kind.

He said, 'Shirley's eleven, but don't tell, she'll get kicked out.'

I started laughing then, and I just couldn't stop. Ella started laughing too, but the others just stared at us, thinking we'd gone crazy or something.

'Sorry,' said Ella, 'we're not laughing at you. It's just that you're the same as us. Bessie isn't really fourteen, she's eleven too.'

Carl and Shirley joined in the laughter. 'Where do you live?' they said, and it turned out they were just round the corner from us.

We decided to go upstairs and dance. Ella wasn't so keen and said that she'd just watch. There was a sound system on a small platform, and a red-headed boy of fourteen or so was handling the controls. I recognized him. He was the boy who lived in the house that backed on to ours. He'd been playing with an Alsatian the day we'd taken Jude to hospital. I watched him carefully. I could just see myself doing that. I'd make an excellent DJ because I've got the gift of the gab. He wasn't very good though. He didn't cue the music right, he was always a bit late and there were too many pauses.

'That's Gary,' said Carl. 'He's trouble.'

'What do you mean?' I said.

'You'll find out.'

'Just keep out of his way,' added Shirley, but she wouldn't say anything more.

Someone relieved Gary at the controls and the music improved. Now it was soul, with a heavy beat. I started to dance. Shirley and Carl were dancing too. We were good. People were watching us. I let myself go with the music. It was loud. I could feel the bass through the floorboards. I moved faster, then faster still, always in time to the beat. It was such a feeling of freedom, just going with the music, losing yourself in it, forgetting everything. Then suddenly, a voice behind me said, 'Hey, not bad. You got rhythm. All you black kids have, it's in the blood.' I turned round and saw Gary standing there. He made whooping sounds and circled the room with large hopping steps.

I stopped dancing. 'I just like to do it,' I said angrily. 'It's got nothing to do with colour.'

'OK, OK, stay cool, I didn't mean anything.'

'Not much you didn't,' said Carl.

I started dancing again, but I wasn't so happy any more. Why do people always decide things about you just because of the way you look?

Shirley put her hand on my shoulder. 'Just ignore him,' she said. 'He's pig-ignorant.'

Ella was coming across the room to join us. I smiled to myself. She'd soon put paid to the idea that all black kids could dance. She moved like a duck on ice. My good mood began to return. It had been such a good evening, and I wasn't going to let pig-ignorant Gary spoil anything. Even when eight o'clock came and Dad arrived with Jude to walk us home, I was still on a high. Carl had said we could go round to their house some time, listen to music, play some games. I didn't care what Dad said, he'd have to let us go, I wouldn't take no for an answer. It was the first good time we'd had in London. I was determined to hang on to it.

Six

I awoke with a start. I could hear dogs barking in the opposite yard, so I looked out of the window. It was still dark, I couldn't see anything but shadows. Was something happening over there or were the animals just amusing themselves? The noise subsided. I was so tired I could hardly see straight, but I was also restless, I couldn't relax, so I got up and went down to the kitchen. The clock on the wall said 3 a. m. No wonder I was tired.

I felt thirsty, so I got myself some water. As I was rinsing out the glass, I heard a strange scraping sound. I stood very still and listened, almost too frightened to breathe. The noise became louder, and then, suddenly, a mouse shot out of the corner by the cooker and scurried across the room, disappearing into a small hole by the kitchen door. Now that I knew what it was, I was no longer afraid. The mouse had moved fast, but I had seen that it was small and brown and cute, with a long, thin tail. I wondered if you could have a house mouse as a pet. Now that we no longer had Jim, it would be fun to have another animal to hold and to play with. I went over to the hole in the hope that the creature would reappear. I turned off the light and waited for a long time, but nothing happened. Maybe the mouse had just been passing through. It was a disappointing thought.

I opened a packet of digestive biscuits in the hope of encouraging more mouse activity, but still there was nothing. At least the mouse was a distraction from the boredom of being unable to sleep and the tendency to churn over things that this produced. Ella's worries were starting to seep into my awareness of things. What would happen if Dad continued to let things slide? How would we cope? I swapped my glass of water for a glass of milk in the hope that this would calm me. Then I went back upstairs to bed.

'This house is ver-min-ous,' I announced, breaking the word into three separate parts so that I didn't make a fool of myself by mispronouncing it.

'What are you talking about?' Dad asked, looking at me crossly.

I tried to stretch my legs along the edge of the sofa, but Ella nudged me to stop wriggling so I sat straight again, wishing the house was less cramped.

'What's verminous?' asked Jude.

Dad took another sip of coffee. His hands were shaking. I wished I'd kept my mouth shut.

'What do you mean, verminous?' asked Dad again.

'Nothing,' I said. 'It was just a joke.'

'Some joke,' said Ella, who obviously knew what verminous meant. She looked shaky too.

'Were you really joking?' asked Dad.

I gave in. 'It was only one, that's all.'

'One what?'

'A mouse.'

Dad groaned. 'That's all we need. What size was it?'

I extended my thumb and forefinger a little. 'Pretty small,' I said.

'Are you sure?'

'Yes. Why? What size are they usually?'

'Dad's worried it might have been a rat,' said Ella astutely.

'Of course it wasn't a rat. If it had been a rat, I'd have been screaming.'

'You're not the only one,' said Ella, in muffled tones.

'It was quite cute. How long do you think it takes to train them? Maybe I could have a mouse circus.'

Ella rolled her eyes. 'Sometimes I think you're mental,' she said. 'Now we've got to live with mice creeping everywhere and getting in the food and in the bedclothes and . . .' a tear rolled down Ella's cheek at the thought. She began to shiver.

'Look, it was only small, I promise.'

'Couldn't you have kept quiet about it?' snapped Dad. 'Look at Ella! Look at Jude!'

I looked. The two of them were crying uncontrollably. 'What's wrong with mice?' I asked, all innocence.

'I don't like mice,' sniffled Ella, 'and I think it's disgusting of you to gloat about it.'

'I only said –'

'Just shut up!'

'Make me!'

'I will in a minute. You don't care about anyone except yourself!'

Dad stood up. 'Be quiet, the pair of you! I can't have a moment's peace, can I? I'm sick to death of the lot of you!' He left the room, slamming the door after him.

'Now look what you've done,' said Ella. 'I've been asking you to behave so he wouldn't get upset but you just went on and on.'

'It wasn't my fault, it was yours. I'm not so stupid as to cry about mice.'

'No, you cry about itsy bitsy spiders instead.'

I was silent for a moment. It hadn't occurred to me that Ella could hate mice the way I hated spiders. I began to feel mean for treating them as a joke, but I hadn't really thought that anyone would mind, much less be afraid. I looked at Jude again. She was rubbing her eyes with a worn-out handkerchief. An elderly friend of Mum's had given her a box with nursery rhyme characters printed on them. They were edged with lace. It was the only time any of us had had real handkerchiefs, not just paper tissues, so Jude always saved them for mopping up tears. They made her feel special.

'I'm sorry, all right?' I said ungraciously.

Ella smiled shakily. She was always pleased when I did the right thing and said sorry, which mostly made apologies stick in my craw.

I went upstairs and found the book I was reading. I pulled off my slippers and curled up in my bed, pulling the blankets round me. I was on page fifty-two, near the end of a chapter, and I was dying to know what would happen next. It was a good story, about a girl who was accused of a crime she hadn't committed. I knew all about that, it happened to me all the time. Every few pages, I paused and listened, hoping that Dad had come out of his room and gone downstairs again, but there was only silence. Maybe he wouldn't come out. Sometimes, he shut himself away for days, and emerged looking unshaven and not quite clean. I hated that more than anything. It was as if I was in Wonderland, like Alice, and nothing was as it should be. I didn't know anyone else whose father behaved like that, it shamed and embarrassed me. Maybe it was an illness, but it didn't seem like one. He didn't cough or wheeze or limp. Why couldn't he try harder to be like other people? The way he behaved was odd, not normal. I was starting to see normal as the most important word in the dictionary. I loved normal, I'd have given anything to have it. Normal was two parents, not just one. It was a father who had a job. It was regular meals that you didn't have to cook yourself, and clean clothes, freshly ironed. It was being allowed to go out on your own without fuss and rows. It was having a dad who always knew what was happening, who didn't have moods, who wasn't depressed, who always spoke to you when you spoke to him. And most of all, normal was not being scared about the future.

I closed my book. I needed to find out what Dad was doing. I passed Jude and Ella's room. They were playing snakes and ladders. Ella was letting

Jude win, I knew that without even being there. She was so good it was vomit-making. I gestured rudely at the door and continued along the passage until I reached Dad's room. It was absolutely quiet. I knocked, but there wasn't an answer. 'Dad, are you in there?' I said.

Silence still. What was he doing? Was he just sitting there, or was something unimaginable going on? I knocked again, more urgently now. 'Dad, it's me,' I said. 'Can I come in?'

'Go away, Bess, leave me alone.'

At least he was still alive in there, but his answer made me cross. Fathers should be looking after their children, not shutting themselves away in their rooms as if they were ten. 'Dad, let me in,' I said. I banged on the door again. 'Come on, Dad, please.'

I was sounding a bit panicky, I knew I was, and I wasn't sorry because it seemed like a good tactic, one which might get him to come out. For a moment, it looked as if nothing was going to happen. Then the door opened slowly. Dad didn't look at me, he just said, 'What do you want?'

'I wanted to know if you were all right.'

'Of course I'm all right.'

Ella and Jude appeared. 'Are you OK, Dad?' said Ella.

'I've just said I am, haven't I? All I want is five minute's peace from you kids, so go away and leave me alone.'

I couldn't help it, I smiled. He was sounding the way I sound when I'm in a bad mood, not like a grown-up at all.

'We were just worried,' said Ella.

'Well, you don't need to be.'

His tone wasn't irritable now, it was gentle and sad, which made me feel sad too, so I said, 'Dad, I'm sorry I told you about the mouse.'

He sighed. 'You were right to tell me, I am your dad. If you can't tell me things, what's the point . . . ?'

I was surprised at this. He was saying we should tell him things, but he always behaved as if we shouldn't. It was confusing. 'Sorry,' I said again.

'I'm not really scared of mice,' said Ella, but even before the words were out, tears of fright began to trickle down her cheeks. 'I'm not scared,' she said again, even more loudly than before. 'I'm crying because . . .' But she couldn't find a good enough excuse.

Dad said, 'I'll have to phone the council and we'll have them round with all the dirt and the mess. They'll probably say it's my fault, that I haven't been clean enough and that's why we've got them, but we did clean everything, didn't we?'

I nodded, though Ella had cleaned most of it.

'I wish your mother was here,' said Dad.

'I know,' said Ella, 'I do too,' and she began to cry again, and Jude did the same and because crying's catching, I started crying too. But then because it was all so awful and miserable and we all looked so stupid, and because there's only so much crying you can do about things anyway, I began to laugh instead, and then Dad laughed and then Jude and Ella, and suddenly we were all laughing, and then it was as if we couldn't stop.

'Everything's so horrible,' I said, with a tearful gurgle. 'I hate it here.'

'So do I,' laughed Jude. 'It stinks.'

'We should have stayed in Leeds,' said Dad. 'I thought I was doing things for the best, bringing you here, giving you a clean break from all the memories, but maybe we should have stayed put.'

'It's not too late,' I said excitedly. 'We could move again, we might even be able to get the old house back.'

Dad sighed. 'It is too late, Bess. The move cost us and anyhow, there isn't any work up there. I'm sure being here will make a difference, it must, it's something we should all hold on to, it'll keep us going now that there's nothing to . . .'

I wondered how the sentence had been going to end. Now that there's nothing to what? Nothing to do? Nothing to feel all right about? *What?* Unusually for me, I didn't plunge in with both feet and ask. I suppose I was scared of the answer. I couldn't manage to keep absolutely quiet though. 'But it's more expensive to live here in London, you said that yourself. If we went back to Leeds, I'm sure you'd get another job, and we'd all be happier and –'

'Bessie, let it go, will you? We are here, and that's that. Let's try to make the best of it. At least you were doing some positive thinking a moment ago with your mouse circus.'

We all laughed again, but it was uneasy laughter. We still felt pretty tense.

'Can I have a biscuit?' asked Jude.

'Tidy up a bit first, you've left your toys all over the place.'

Jude began to grumble, but then she seemed to remember all the tears because she stopped abruptly and went into the living-room. I followed. She began to pile her toys and books in a tottering column which I took from her crossly, telling her to watch what she was doing or she'd break the lot and then there'd be even more crying.

Dad said, 'Bess, take Jude upstairs and play with her for a while, will you?'

'Oh Dad, can't Ella? I've got some drawing I want to do.'

'Ella does enough around here. You spend all your time sliding out of chores. Don't think I haven't noticed.'

'I do my share, Dad, I'm just quick, that's all, so no one ever sees me.'

'Nice try, Bess,' said Dad. At least he was smiling.

'It's true, don't you believe me?'

'You kids, you're driving me crazy. Just do it, will you?'

I didn't want to send Dad fleeing up to his room again, so I stopped arguing and steered Jude upstairs. 'What do you want to play then?' I asked her. 'You could do some drawing with me. Tell you what, let's draw the mouse circus.'

'I don't want to think about mice.'

'Yes you do, it'll be fun, you won't feel so scared of them. Look, I'll start with the ringmaster mouse. His name's Frank and he's got a moustache.'

'Mice don't have moustaches.'

'This one did, I saw.'

Jude giggled. 'It didn't.'

'You wait until you see him, then you'll know.'

'I don't want to see him.'

'Yes you do, he's really, really good, you'll like him such a lot.'

'Why was Ella crying about him then?'

'Some people are afraid of mice, but it's silly, mice can't hurt you.' I remembered then that spiders couldn't hurt you either, but that didn't stop me worrying about them.

'Dad said mice were dirty.'

'They might be a bit, but we could clean them.'

'How?'

'With a bucket and soapy water. It's the first stage of the training. Look, I'll draw a bucket.'

As I crayoned in the yellow bucket and the light brown mice with spotted waistcoats and big black moustaches, I knew how stupid I'd been to mention mice at all. I should have thought first, I shouldn't just have said it. I probably wouldn't have, or at least, not like that, if I hadn't been so keen to bring the word 'verminous' into a conversation and show everyone how clever I was.

As I played with Jude, creating obstacle courses for mice, I found that time passed more quickly than it had done for days. I wondered if maybe Ella was right, and we would be better off at school after all. I thought of Shirley and Carl and wondered if I'd be going to the same school as them. What would it be like? Big, I knew that, bigger than the one in Leeds. And everyone would probably look down on me because southerners always looked down on people from up north. At Claremont Road, I'd been the best in the class at drawing, but I hadn't been much good at anything else. Nothing else had interested me much, though I'd quite liked reading. They'd probably be doing different lessons at the new school that I wouldn't understand and I'd look thick and boring. I'd had lots of friends at my old school but the move had been so sudden, I'd hardly even had a chance to say goodbye, and now I was going to a new school, most probably in the middle of a term.

And supposing, just supposing, that after all this, Dad never got a job and never felt any better? It would all have been for nothing. If only Mum was here, I thought, and my breathing became more shallow as I felt the sickness in my stomach.

'I'm drawing the cat now, the one that helps train the mice,' said Jude.

'That's good,' I said absently, from the other corner of the room.

'I could make the cat look quite friendly, so the mice wouldn't be scared. Or I could make him fierce so that he could train them better.'

'Whatever.'

'Listen properly, Bessie.'

'I am listening.'

'No you're not, you're thinking,' said Jude accusingly. 'What are you thinking about?'

'Mum,' I answered. I wasn't sure how much I should say to Jude, who was only a little kid after all, but she didn't seem to mind talking about Mum the way that Ella sometimes did.

'I think about her a lot too. She won't be coming back again, will she?'

'No,' I answered softly. The thought intensified my sadness. It made me think of the music Mum always used to listen to. She called it the blues, and it was sad music, music to think by, and it was Mum's favourite kind. I remember that whenever Mum caught me looking lost or miserable, she would say, 'Got the blues, Bessie?' and whenever she said this, I would feel better because I knew Mum understood. It's funny that music can be a colour, and that feelings can be a colour too. I took a blue crayon and shaded over my sheet of paper. It was a good colour, blue. In a funny sort of way, looking at it helped me to make sense of things.

Seven

On Saturday morning, there was a knock at the door. We were in our pyjamas, even though it was half past ten. Dad was still in bed. 'I'll answer it,' I said, running downstairs.

'No, leave it!' Dad shouted from his room, so I knew he was awake. I stood by the door. It was obvious that we were in, the person outside must have heard Dad yelling. The flap on the letter-box clattered up and I saw a pair of eyes peering through. I crouched and peered back. It was funny, looking into someone else's eyes through the narrow slit, and I couldn't help laughing. The person on the other side laughed too and said, 'Bessie?'

'Yes, it's me,' I replied, still not opening the door. 'Who are you?'

'It's Shirley, from the club. Aren't you going to let me in?'

'My dad said I couldn't.'

'I came to ask if you and Ella could come round.'

'Wait there,' I said, 'I'll find out.'

It took me ages to convince Dad that we wouldn't come to any harm playing with Carl and Shirley. He wanted to know all sorts of stupid things such as whether they were well-behaved and what their parents were like. I tried to stay calm as he questioned me, because I knew that if I got cross, he'd say no straight away, but the effort of holding myself in was so great that I began to feel like exploding. Eventually, he said yes, obviously wanting to end the discussion. I decided there was something to be said for Dad's low moods. If I persisted for long enough, he stopped trying.

I was surprised to see Shirley still standing on the step when I finally opened the door. I gave her lots of points for patience. 'We can come but we've got to get dressed,' I said. 'Do you want to come in?'

Shirley shook her head. 'Come round to our place when you're ready,' she said, and strolled off.

Ella was surprised that Shirley had come. She'd thought they'd forget all about us. I suppose it was nice to be remembered. It eased some of the fed-upness we'd been feeling.

As we walked up the street, Ella said, 'What if I say something stupid and they decide they don't want to know us?'

I didn't have much patience with Ella when she was like this. 'Of course they'll want to know us whatever we say,' I answered.

'They might think . . . well, I don't know. They just might not like us.'

'They won't like us if you go all pathetic and feeble.'

Ella shut up then, and we arrived at Carl and Shirley's place in silence.

A tall woman wearing tailored trousers and a loose, cerise-coloured top opened the door. Our mum had always looked smart, but this woman was glamorous, like a model. I envied Carl and Shirley. She smiled at us and invited us in, asking our names. I had to tell her – Ella was tongue-tied as always.

Shirley and Carl came up the hall to meet us. Carl grinned at Ella and Shirley put her arm round me as if we'd been friends for ever. 'Can we go upstairs?' Carl said.

'Sure,' said their mother. 'Help yourselves to lemonade and biscuits.'

'Come on,' said Shirley, shoving her way through the kitchen door. It was the same size and shape as ours, but it seemed to belong to a different world. There were fitted units, with doors that were guaranteed to stay on their hinges. The floor was tiled in black and white checks, the way it is in ads for the stuff that kills all known germs. You could see your reflection in it. There was a large fridge freezer, and as Shirley opened it I caught a glimpse of all the things I like best in the world to eat – chocolate mousses, Mini Baby Bel cheeses, cans of Coke and ginger beer, and Marks & Spencer's pizza. My envy increased.

We each took a can to drink and Carl laid out a plateful of chocolate biscuits. We followed Carl upstairs. 'We'll go in Shirley's room, it's bigger,' he said. At the end of the landing there was a staircase, like a ladder but wider. We went up and found ourselves in an attic room with a sloping ceiling and windows that covered one of the walls. I went across and looked out. From here, you could see for miles, all along the roofs of the houses. The streets were spread beneath us like toy town, small and compact. There was a railway line in the distance, and trains snaked along it, reminding me of my train set. Beyond that, there were trees, and a church with a spire.

Shirley stood beside me. 'That spire got struck by lightning once. I was up here, looking out, and I saw it.'

'What happened?' I said, but she wouldn't describe it. I don't think she'd really seen it at all.

'What's it like here on firework night?' I asked.

'Amazing,' said Shirley. 'You'll have to come round, it's not far off now. Do you want to play some computer games? We've got tons of them. Or we could play some music. I've got a new CD.'

I liked listening to Shirley's music. She had taste. She liked strong voices and a smooth rhythm. After a while, Carl and Ella went off somewhere by themselves. Shirley and I sprawled on the floor, discovering that we both knew about the blues – the music and the feeling. It was something else we had in common.

'Dad's home,' said Shirley, sitting up suddenly. She went to the window. 'That's his car, the green one. I always hear it. He did this room for me. It's a loft conversion, I only had a box room before. He's a builder. What does your dad do?'

I hesitated for a moment. Then I said, 'He's ill. He's not at work at the moment.'

'What about your mum? Does she work?'

There was a long silence. I wasn't sure if I could

75

tell her about Mum, I didn't know her well enough yet. So I just didn't answer, I started playing with the fluffy toy cat that lay across the end of Shirley's bed. I pretended it was Jim.

'Is something wrong?' asked Shirley.

'No,' I said.

'Sorry, I know I'm nosy. Mum's always giving me stick for it. I didn't mean anything.'

'It's OK, I know you didn't.' And then suddenly I said, 'Mum died a few months ago. At Christmas.'

I was afraid that Shirley would be embarrassed or upset or something, but she just said, 'Oh.' There was another silence. I went on playing with the cat that looked like Jim. Then Shirley said, 'My Gran died last year. I still wish she was here.' And that was all. But I knew that she understood, and I also knew that she was a proper friend, even though I hadn't known her very long. She was someone I could trust.

Ella and Carl returned, and we began a game of cards. Normally I'm good, and I really wanted to show Shirley what I could do, but from the start it didn't go right and I lost hand after hand. To make matters worse, Ella was the one who was winning. I mean, she never wins normally, it was hard to believe, but there she was playing like a river-boat gambler, all poker-faced and cleaning us out. I could have cried, but instead, I got crosser and crosser. Carl muttered something about bad losers, and that made me madder than ever. I snatched the cards out of Ella's hands and threw them on the floor. There was a shocked silence. Then I burst into tears.

It was weird, I was expecting everyone to be really angry with me then, but instead Carl and Shirley told the story of the time they were staying with cousins of theirs who beat them at everything, and how they'd run out of the house at ten o'clock at night, and the police had been called to find them. I forgot how upset I was then and started laughing, and they laughed too, and soon we were all laughing to the point where Ella got hiccups and had to drink out of the wrong side of a glass.

'Do you want to see our mice?' asked Shirley.

'*Mice?*' said Ella, turning pale.

'Pet mice,' said Carl. 'You're not scared of them, are you?'

So we learnt how to hold white mice and to stroke them and to feed them bits of bread and cheese, and all the while, Ella was turning paler and paler, but she didn't let on, and we didn't say a thing about the mice we had at home, and after a time, even Ella sort of got to like them, or at least, not to mind so much.

Shirley let me try on some of her clothes. She was slightly bigger than me, which I was pleased about. I'd seldom met anyone of my own age who wasn't stunted. She had good taste in clothes, and as I changed in and out of her numerous pairs of jeans and tops, she told me that their mother was a fashion designer who had her own stall at one of the markets. I wasn't surprised. Usually, kids' mothers dress to embarrass, with skirts that are too long or jeans that are too tight. Although I'd only seen her briefly, I knew that Carl and Shirley's mum would always look just right.

'Do you want a makeover?' Shirley asked Ella.

I could tell that she didn't want one; Ella was always self-conscious.

'Go on,' said Shirley. 'I'm very good, I'm going to get into fashion when I grow up, like Mum.'

'She doesn't want to. Let her alone,' said Carl.

'She does want to, don't you Ella?' Shirley said, and of course Ella agreed. She was such a pushover.

I squatted on the floor with Carl and continued to play with the mice, while Shirley sat Ella on a stool and got out a make-up box. She laid out several lipsticks and a tube of mascara. 'You've got good bone structure,' said Shirley, looking at her critically. 'You're so lucky.'

Ella smiled. I don't think she knew what good bone structure was, but Shirley made it sound worth having. Ella turned her face to the light and let Shirley brush it with foundation and blusher. 'What's that for?' she asked, pointing to a small tube.

'It's highlighter,' said Shirley, putting little dabs of blue on Ella's eyelids. 'Look at her, Carl, it suits her, doesn't it?'

Carl looked. 'She always looks nice,' he said shyly, and Ella's colour deepened.

By the time Shirley had finished with her, Ella did look different. She looked older and less scared. I couldn't have put it into words then, but I think I felt sorry for Ella at that moment. Somewhere in the back of my mind, I realized how uncertain she felt about everything and how little belief she had in herself. We used to get reports at the end of the year from school, and Ella's had always said the same thing: *Ella is very able but she lacks self-confidence.* My reports, of course, said almost the exact opposite. And as she sat there, sort of pleased with the way she looked, and sort of worried in case we were all secretly laughing at her, I wished that she'd get tougher and be more like me, because I don't care what anybody thinks, or at least, not so as you'd notice.

'There,' said Shirley, stepping back to admire her work.

Ella turned to me and said, 'Do you think I could wear this home or would Dad think I shouldn't?'

'Our dad wouldn't care, but Mum would kill Shirley for going out with makeup on,' said Carl. 'Mothers are always trickier than fathers if you ask me. Dad doesn't notice anything, but Mum always does.'

Ella obviously hadn't told Carl about Mum. She said nothing. She just picked up a lipstick and pulled off the top. She dabbed it on the back of her hand. It was a deep red-brown, the shade of autumn chrysanthemums.

'What's the matter?' asked Carl, obviously aware from the meaningful silence that something was going on.

'Nothing,' Ella answered, but she looked as if she felt like crying.

I said hastily, 'I think we'd better be getting home

now. We told Dad we wouldn't stay out too long.'

Ella flashed me a grateful look, and I decided it would have been better all round if I'd been born the oldest. I'm a much more coping sort of person. I understood how Ella felt just then, but at the same time I couldn't help being fed up with her for spoiling the afternoon. We could have stayed, got away from Dad and that drab, miserable house for a while longer. As we walked home, I couldn't stop myself jostling her. I made it look like an accident, but I did it on purpose. That's the trouble with sisters. They bring out the worst in you.

Eight

The television arrived. Ella, Jude and I gathered round it worshipfully, to watch it being installed. It would, I was certain, make London seem more like home. The black box, with its shiny screen, seemed to promise that things would get back to normal.

We had it on all day. I half expected Dad to insist that we turned it off and found something else to do, but he barely seemed to notice. We ate our dinner on trays that evening, while watching the news.

Ella kept checking the time. Jude was usually in bed by now, but Dad was sitting in the big chair, half asleep. I could tell that Ella was wondering if she'd have to be the one to bath Jude. I knew I wasn't doing it. I planned to watch *Coronation Street*.

A holiday programme came on, reminding me suddenly of summers when we'd gone to Spain. We'd even been to Italy once, and seen lots of famous paintings and eaten ice-cream. At the Vatican, they'd had soldiers who looked like Beefeaters, but they'd been dressed with even more colour and style. There had been sunshine and excitement and something new to see each day. Dad had loved it. He'd been so happy then. Mum had too.

Dad had fallen asleep. He was snoring now, so Ella said, 'Dad,' but he didn't reply. She went over and shook him gently. He woke up with a start.

'What's the matter?' he asked.

'Are you all right?' Ella said. She never seemed to stop worrying about him.

'I think I've got some kind of bug, flu or something,' he said.

I wanted to believe it was flu, because flu only lasted a few days and then it was gone, but I was afraid it was something that would take much longer to get better. I don't know whether Ella believed him or not, because all she said was, 'Do you think you should go to bed?'

'I should see to Jude.'

Jude briefly took her eyes off the television screen. 'You don't have to, I can see to myself. I'm big now.'

'I'll see to her, Dad,' said Ella, too good to be true as always. She looked at me, so I made it obvious that I had no intention of moving. Ella opened her mouth as if she was going to say something to me and then seemed to change her mind. She steered Jude out of the room and went to run the bath.

'Go and help her, Bessie,' Dad said.

The *Coronation Street* theme tune was just starting to play and I was conducting from the sofa. I gave Dad a look of extreme indignation, but he remained unmoved. 'Do it now, Bess,' he said.

In the bathroom, water was gushing from the taps and Ella was getting out Jude's red and yellow ducks. She obviously thought I'd come to help off my own bat because she gave me this watery smile.

I said, 'Look, you don't really need me, do you? *Coronation Street*'s on.'

'No, stay, Bess, please.' She lowered her voice so that Jude wouldn't hear. 'He's getting ill, isn't he?'

I shrugged noncommittally. No sense in getting Ella more worked up than she already was.

'I don't think I can handle any more of this. It's like drowning,' she said, breathlessly, trailing her fingers through the bathwater.

'I expect it'll be OK,' I said, wishing she'd stop going on about how awful everything was all the time.

'You don't care, do you?'

'Of course I care, I just don't see the point in getting into a state about it. What with you and Dad, there's one drama after another.'

Ella pulled off Jude's dress with none of her usual gentleness and then her vest and pants.

'What's the matter?' Jude asked.

'Nothing.'

'Are you cross?'

'No.'

'You seem cross.'

'Well, I'm not, OK?'

Jude opened her mouth as if she was about to produce evidence of Ella's crossness but then seemed to change her mind and jumped into the bath with a huge splash that wet Ella's jeans right through. I started to laugh, but Ella yelled, 'You little brat!'

'I didn't mean it,' said Jude.

'Yes you did,' said Ella, removing the ducks and putting them on the highest shelf. 'You're not playing now.'

'Oh please!'

'And you can stop laughing too, Bessie, because you're going to have to finish her.'

'I don't want Bess, I want you!' said Jude.

'Then you should have behaved,' said Ella.

Jude hit the water with her hands and sent it splattering in Ella's face and up the wall behind her. Ella grabbed her hands and held them together.

'You're hurting me,' said Jude.

'I don't care. It serves you right.'

The door opened. Dad stood there looking at all three of us. 'You have to have someone running round you all the time, don't you?' he said.

'Ella's in a bad mood,' said Jude.

'Jude splashed everywhere on purpose.'

'I never!'

'You did!'

'For heaven's sake, my head feels like it's going to burst and all you can do is argue.'

We fell silent and looked guilty. Dad did look ill, he was a funny colour and his eyes were nearly closing.

Ella said, 'Sorry, Dad, go on up to bed. I'll clear up.'

'No, I'll do it. You can't be trusted.'

84

'I can, honestly.'

'Go back downstairs, Ella. You too, Bessie. You've got what you wanted now, you can watch television until your eyes drop out.'

We went back to the living room. *Coronation Street* was finishing, but I wasn't bothered any more. Ella wasn't speaking to me. I should have been relieved, but I wasn't. I hate that kind of disapproving silence, it's horrible, really torturing. Dad was silent like that all the time.

Eventually I decided to go to bed. All the good programmes were finished, and there was only a documentary and some golfing highlights.

'Goodnight, then,' I said to Ella.

She turned her back on me as I went upstairs.

Late next morning, I went into Dad's room with Ella. He was still asleep, but he was tossing and turning. Ella put her hand on his forehead, the way Mum always used to do with us to check if we had a temperature. Ella was very quiet and gentle but her touch woke Dad up.

'Do you want me to get the doctor?' Ella asked.

'We haven't got one here, I haven't had a chance to sort it out. Besides, Ella, if a doctor thought I couldn't look after you properly, they might want you to stay with somebody else.'

'Who?' I said, suddenly afraid.

'Foster-parents. Even a home.'

I went cold. That possibility had been at the back of my mind for weeks, put there by Ella mostly, but I'd told myself that I was being silly, that it couldn't happen. Now I began to see why Ella had been so worried.

She bit the tips of her fingers. 'What shall I do then?' she asked.

'Nothing. Just keep the others occupied and give them breakfast. There's baked beans and some bread for lunchtime. You'll be OK.'

'What about you?'

'I don't want anything. You know what they say, "Feed a cold, starve a fever."'

'Dad –'

'I just want to sleep, OK?'

We went downstairs and Ella put the breakfast things on the table. There wasn't enough bread for both breakfast and dinner, so we just had corn-flakes. I didn't feel full up enough, but Ella said we had to tighten our belts. This wasn't very fair – she never wants as much to eat as I do, so mine was the only belt being tightened as far as I could see.

That was the start of one of the longest days I've ever known. Jude tried to be good and I tried too. Ella heated the beans for dinner, but they stuck to the bottom of the saucepan in a globby mess that she couldn't scrape off. She burnt the toast, so I ate it and her and Jude had cracker biscuits instead.

Time dragged. The television didn't seem so interesting now that we'd finally got one. I did more of the jigsaw puzzle I'd been working on and Ella read, but I knew she wasn't concentrating, she kept going up to check on Dad. She would stand by his bed and listen for his breathing. He was so still and quiet that both of us were scared, he seemed such a long way off. Ella said he wasn't actually sleeping, but he might as well have been. He wasn't talking or eating or drinking. He seemed to have gone into another world and left us behind. Ella said she hoped this wouldn't go on for too much longer because if it did, something would have to be done, and she didn't know what. How do you find a doctor if you don't have one? We weren't even on the phone. It would mean going to a call-box, and neither of us had ever had to use one before so we didn't know how. And what if Dad was right and the doctor decided that he wasn't fit to look after us? What would happen then?

Ella sent me to the corner shop to get some bread. As I was opening the front door, the light bulb on the landing went out with a pinging sound, and the stairs were suddenly dark. We looked everywhere but we couldn't find another bulb, and anyway, we weren't even sure how to change one, so the darkness remained. Jude wouldn't go up or down the stairs on her own, so every time she wanted to go to the bathroom or to fetch a toy, one of us had to go with her. I could tell that Ella's panic was starting to grow. She kept saying, 'If Dad doesn't get better, what will we do?' We all sat in my room because it was near Dad's, and we put the radio on so that there was a grown-up voice to listen to.

Ella talked a lot too. I think she was trying to fill the silences. Then she told me something that was odd. She said, 'You know, Bess, I thought that if I managed everything all the time and kept on being good and calm and kind, the fates, or God or whatever it was that sorted out these things, would make Dad happy and then everything would slide back into place as if the bad things had never happened. But I also knew, you see, that if I got it wrong even once, that would be the end of everything, and nothing would ever be the same again.'

'Did you mess it up then?' asked Jude.

Ella looked sad. 'I think I must have done,' she said.

'That's not true, Ella, it can't be,' I said, though I wasn't really sure, it's hard to know if it's possible to stop bad things or not.

But Ella said, 'In a way, not being able to stop them's even worse. It would be terrible to think there's nothing I can do.'

I thought I knew what she meant, and it occurred to me that perhaps Ella had to be good, she couldn't really help herself, so maybe it wasn't fair to blame her for it.

Ella didn't go to bed until very late, it was after eleven. And several times in the night, I heard her checking on Dad.

Next morning, things were much the same. As Ella and I went into the room, we saw that although Dad's eyes were open, he didn't seem to know what was happening. He didn't reply to any of Ella's questions – he seemed not to hear. We sat on his bed and tried to work out what was happening. Was it flu? Ella tried to give Dad aspirin with some water but he wouldn't take it. Ella cried then, and I did too, a bit, but tears didn't make any difference because there were no grown-ups there to make it better.

We wandered in and out of his room, hoping to see some change. Between times, we sat on the stairs and tried to think what we should do. Eventually, Ella said, 'Bess, I think we have to ring for an ambulance.'

I took a deep breath. I could hardly believe that Ella was saying it. 'Is it really that bad?' I asked.

'I don't know,' said Ella. 'Don't you see? That's the whole problem. I just don't know.'

She was crying now. 'It'll be all right,' I said. 'Look, I'll do it. You don't have to. I'll do it, Ella.'

'You don't mind?'

I did mind, I was scared, but I wasn't going to say so, especially not when Ella looked so relieved, and so pleased with me for once. 'Of course I don't. I'll do it now.'

Ella tipped all the coins she could find into my hand. '999 calls are free,' I said.

'They might tell you to phone somewhere else.'

'No, they don't do that. They have to come if you phone them, I read that somewhere,' I said, but I took the money anyway, just in case.

It took me a while to find a phone. One phone box had all the glass knocked out of it and although the phone seemed all right, I felt so funny with the rain coming in on me through the gaps that I couldn't stay. I knew it was stupid, and that Ella would be waiting and wondering where I was, but I just couldn't help it.

There were two phone boxes outside the post

office in the High Street. They both stank, but I chose the least smelly one. On the wall, there was a list of instructions on how to make a call. I pushed the buttons as fast as I could and a voice asked which service I needed: fire, police, or ambulance.

'Ambulance,' I answered.

The voice said, 'What's the address, love?' and suddenly, I thought what if we were wrong and it wasn't an emergency at all? What would they do to us? And Dad had said he didn't need a doctor, it was almost the only thing he had said since he'd been ill. But, most of all, I didn't want anyone to think he wasn't a good father to us. I hung up the phone.

At once, I wished I hadn't. How would I tell Ella that I'd messed it up and no help would be coming after all? What if Dad died because of me? You could die of all sorts of things, even flu, people did, all the time. I ran out of the phone box. Supposing someone was trying to trace my call? I'd seen it in detective films. If you dialled 999 and didn't say who you were, they could find out where the call had been made from and come and get you. I ran all the way home.

As I slammed the front door shut, I half hoped they would come after me, because then everything would have been solved for us and we wouldn't have to worry about what to do any more. Jude and Ella were sitting in darkness at the top of the stairs. They'd been waiting for me to come home.

'Is the ambulance coming?' asked Ella.

I shook my head. After all my brave talk, I hadn't

been able to deliver. 'I couldn't do it,' I said. 'I'm sorry.' I sat on the stairs beside them.

There was silence for a moment. Then Ella said, 'It's OK, I shouldn't have sent you. I'm the oldest. I should have done it. It was my responsibility.'

I was cross with her for being so understanding. 'I said I would. *I* should have done it.'

Ella sighed. 'Don't worry,' she said. 'Anyway, he may get better by himself.'

We went into the living-room where the television was blaring. We started to watch a film. It was for grown-ups and I didn't understand what it was about, but sitting in front of it made things seem more ordinary.

And the funny thing was, later that evening, Dad did seem better. He ate some biscuits and drank a glass of water and swallowed the aspirin Ella gave him. Then he slept, real sleep, Ella said, not pretend sleep like before. We watched him for a long, long time, just in case, but nothing bad happened and it seemed safe for us to go to bed.

'Goodnight, Bess,' Ella said. 'I'm glad you couldn't make the call.'

I was glad too, but trust Ella to be so good that she actually said it. Why couldn't she hold a grudge like any normal person? I was trying to like her, but she made it hard, she really did.

Nine

I was watching television yet again. It was all we ever did, apart from reading and drawing and jigsaw puzzles. I was absorbed in a game show, and trying to figure out the answers before the contestants did. I wasn't doing well enough. So far I'd only got two right. It made me feel stupid, but I couldn't quit in case I hit the winning streak that would make me feel clever again.

Ella didn't like quizzes, so she was upstairs brooding until it was over. Jude had gone up too. She only liked cartoons and other baby programmes. I looked at the clock on the mantelpiece. It was nearly half past one already. Time was crawling by.

I was suddenly distracted. Dad was coming down the stairs in a faded tracksuit. He hadn't shaved and his hair wasn't combed, but I was relieved to see him. He had been in bed for four days now, and I had started to be afraid that he would never get up again.

'Where are the others?' he asked.

I explained with one eye on the television. A series of pictures came up on the screen and my interest in the show increased. 'Which is the odd one out?' said the show's host. I squinted at a row of faces. I wasn't sure.

'Looks like you need glasses,' said Dad.

I was glad he was behaving normally again, but I hated the idea of glasses. How could you look glamorous and interesting in a pair of specs? For the first time, I was pleased that money was short. If I did need them, it would be ages before we could afford them. As if he was reading my mind, Dad said, 'Eye tests are still free for kids. And you can get NHS glasses that don't cost anything.'

I pretended I hadn't heard. Ordinary glasses were bad enough, but the kind that were free would be so awful it just wasn't true. Dad said, 'Isn't there something else on?' so I reluctantly switched channels and got an American sitcom.

'Is everything OK?' asked Dad.

'Yes,' I said, though it wasn't. Dad had been out of action for days. How could everything be OK?

Dad watched the sitcom to the end. Then he said, 'There's some kind of family fun thing in the park for Guy Fawkes. It starts later this afternoon, I heard it on the radio. Do you want to go?'

Often when Dad came out of one of his bad patches he liked us all to have a good time. It was as if he wanted to make up for it. I needed to get out – I was sick to death of being in the house, but I wasn't sure how Dad would be if we went. He might not comb his hair or remember to put smart clothes on. So all I said was, 'Yes, we could go,' though my voice was harder than I'd meant it to be.

Dad said, 'Are you angry about something?'

'No,' I answered, though of course I was angry about a lot of things. I wished Dad would try harder to keep things going. Didn't he know what it was like for us when he got into one of his stupid moods?

Jude came tearing down the stairs at that moment, with Ella close behind. Jude flung herself at Dad as she always did and gave him a hug. 'Hi sweetheart,' Dad said. 'Have you been good for Ella?'

Jude nodded. 'Are you better now?' she asked.

Dad said, 'I'm OK,' and me and Ella looked at him closely, hoping it was true. Then he added, 'Come on kids, get ready. We're going out.'

'Are you sure you're well enough?' asked Ella.

I looked at her in surprise. We shared the same worries, then, about being embarrassed by Dad.

The park was ten minutes walk from the house. We went past the lorry yard, and Gary, the boy we'd seen at the club, was outside, teasing an Alsatian that was wheeling round at the end of a piece of string which was tied to a post. He noticed me and Ella, but he didn't say a word, which was probably just as well. If Dad realized he went to the club too, he'd probably put a stop to it. Gary was obviously trying to see what the dog would do if it was provoked enough. He danced towards it with a morsel of something and then away again without allowing the dog to taste it. The distance was finely judged.

'That looks dangerous,' said Dad.

'I'm more worried about the dog,' said Ella. 'It's cruel to tease it like that. I wish Gary would stop doing it.'

'How do you know him?' asked Dad sharply.

'We don't,' I said. 'Carl and Shirley told us the boy who lived round the back was called Gary, that's all.'

Ella seemed about to contradict me, but I glared her into silence.

'Well, make sure you keep away from him, he's a trouble-maker. You can't trust Alsatians at the best of times, and the way that kid's going that dog will be a killer.'

The idea of killer dogs was an interesting variation on Dad's dire warnings. He'd never worried about that before. I kicked a stone across the path. At least he'd shaved, and put on a clean shirt. That was something.

We heard fairground music before we reached the park. Dad said, 'You're going to have to be very grown-up about this and just look. No rides, I can't afford it.'

'Then what was the point of us coming?' I said angrily.

Dad pretended not to hear.

I ran ahead with Jude and came speeding back with a report. 'There are toffee apples and popcorn,' I said.

'And a horse roundabout,' added Jude.

'There's tents, but I can't see what's in them.'

'Two girls my age went past with lion face paint. Can I be a lion?' asked Jude.

95

'We'll see,' said Dad, meaning it would depend on how much it cost.

'I could see a clown, but I don't think there's a circus,' Jude continued. 'He's going round on stilts, collecting for a hospital.'

'There's a brass band playing,' I said in sneering tones.

'It's a song I know,' said Jude, jumping up and down. 'What's it called again?'

We all knew it but we couldn't tell her what it was. Ella began humming it and I joined in. I always stay in tune, whereas Ella squeaks on the high notes.

Up ahead, someone in a rabbit suit was selling programmes. I hurried past him in case he said something to me. I can't stand it when grown-ups get into costumes and pretend to be silly animals. It's so embarrassing.

'Look, there's juggling,' said Ella.

We stopped to watch, our breath smoking in the cold November weather.

'I want to learn that,' I said. 'Remember, in Leeds, there was that place near the canal with juggling stuff? Can I go round by myself, Dad? I won't get lost or anything, promise.'

'Stay with us, Bessie.'

'Please, I'll meet you back here in three-quarters of an hour, nothing can happen to me, really it can't.'

Dad looked round, assessing all potential hazards. 'All right, but be careful and don't go far,' he said.

I was ecstatic. It was weeks since I'd been allowed anywhere on my own. I ran a little way and stopped by the big wheel. It rotated slowly and then gathered speed. The top was nearly in the branches of the trees. I felt in my pockets for any odd coin saved from better times, but they were empty except for my red car, so I pretended to be grown-up and tried to be content with looking. Soon, though, the wish to ride became too much, so I moved on and peered in one of the tents. Stallholders were selling handmade things. There were wooden puzzle games and leather belts and lots of silver jewellery with little blue or yellow stones.

If Mum had been there, she would have bought me a game, I was sure of it. Suddenly, not to be able to have her there or to tell her what was happening was so sad and confusing that I hurried out of the park gates and on to the street. It was strangely quiet here after all the noise and bustle of the fair, though I could still hear the brass band playing in the distance. I looked at the crumbling buildings round me. The doors to several large houses were boarded up, though there were shabby cloths at the windows that functioned as curtains. Small children played in doorways and dogs without collars nosed their way along the street, sniffing at walls and passers-by.

This place was different from my home in Leeds, but I didn't mind it, and I wasn't scared. At least I was out of the house, if only for a little while, and Dad wasn't there to panic about how dangerous it was. It didn't feel at all dangerous, it felt exciting, more than anything. But as I walked along the street, peering in shop windows, I remembered that I'd said I wouldn't go far, and soon it would be time to meet Dad as I'd promised.

It suddenly seemed like a fairy tale, the one where the little girl disobeys her parents and strays off the path and nearly comes to a nasty end. I turned round and ran back to the park.

They were all standing by the hot-dog stand. 'Where have you been?' demanded Dad. 'We've been worried sick.'

'Just up there. I didn't go far. I'm not really late, am I? I couldn't tell what time it was because of my watch. It doesn't have a battery.'

'You promised,' hissed Ella. 'Look what you've done.'

I knew what Ella meant. The improvement in Dad's mood was vanishing. He looked nervy again. 'I couldn't help it,' I said.

Ella gave me a little shove which said I should have helped it, but Ella didn't know everything. She didn't seem to understand what it was like to feel happy and free to roam around where you wanted without grown-ups sniffing after you and telling you that whatever you were doing was dangerous or wrong or upsetting to them in some other way. Trust Dad to get in a state just because I wasn't absolutely dead on time. He spoiled everything. He was stupid and mean. We were all missing Mum, not just him, and it was time he realized it.

As we walked home silently, Jude started snivelling, I don't know why.

Ella said, 'Look at her. This is all your fault.'

I didn't say anything. I gave her my killer look, and prepared myself for the worst Guy Fawkes night ever. Dad wouldn't let us stay in the park for the fireworks, he said it wasn't safe, someone might push us in a bonfire or shove bangers in our trouser pockets, and I couldn't be trusted. I was amazed I'd managed to reach eleven if life was as perilous as that. I went up to my room as soon as I got in, and cried into the pillow.

Just when I thought that my existence would never ever be bearable again, there was a ring at the door. Shirley and Carl were there, asking us to go round again and watch the fireworks from their bedroom window. Dad nearly didn't let me go, but Ella told him she wouldn't enjoy it much without me, so in the end he agreed, though he made us take Jude too.

We sat on the ledge that ran the width of the window and watched glowing sprinkles of light falling out of the sky. Green and red and yellow embers showered to the ground, filling the air with smoke that lingered in our clothes and hair. Shirley sat beside me, gripping my shoulder excitedly every now and then, her face all smiles. Carl was humming to himself. He had a good voice, and once in a while we all joined in, even Jude, though she didn't know the tunes. Ella sat hugging her knees, just staring at the sky. She seemed so calm.

Shirley and Carl's mum came in with plates of spare ribs and little crunchy potatoes. There was popcorn too, and gingerbread men, and Coca Cola to drink, which we sucked through straws. Carl put some music on, and we watched the fireworks chasing one another as if in tune with the rhythm. Shirley said she didn't have a friend outside of school and she wanted us to be best friends for ever and ever. She'd wanted that as soon as she'd seen me. She said we were kindred spirits and we had to promise to stick up for each other through thick and thin.

I took her hand and we went out of the room and sat on the ladder that led to the loft. 'Do you swear that you'll be my friend no matter what?' I said. It seemed important to have her promise, I don't know why. She grinned at me and said, 'For-ever and ever, come hell or high water, I will be Bessie's friend, so there.' We returned to the fire-works blood sisters.

It's funny how you can remember some times in your life as special. That evening was special to me. As we all sat there, it was as if a terrible weight had been lifted. I forgot about Dad. I even put Mum to the back of my mind. It was perfect enjoyment, with no worries and no fears. It was one of the happiest nights of my life.

Ten

Dad was speaking to Ella and Jude from time to time, but he wasn't speaking to me. I knew it was because I'd been late back the day before when we'd gone to the park. I'd said I was sorry – I'd said it twice – but it didn't make any difference. Dad was determined to punish me with his silence.

It was like being put in a big, dark, void where you don't exist to anyone outside. I tried to make him talk to me by starting up conversations with him. I was determined not to let him see that I minded his silence, so I decided to behave as if he was talking to me, and as if we were having normal conversations. I went into bright and breezy mode, cheerfully saying what a nice day it was, and how lucky it was that the sun was shining. There were some really good programmes on television and wouldn't it be interesting to find out how radios actually worked? I told him that when I was a little kid, I used to think there was a very small person scrunched up inside every single one – that was funny of me, wasn't it? Ella told me to shut up and said I shouldn't keep winding Dad up, but I wasn't, I was just trying to get him to stop ignoring me.

It didn't work; he barely said a word. I tried to find out if he was going to let me go to the youth club with Ella that evening. He'd let me go to Shirley's for the fireworks, but if anything he seemed even crosser with me now than he'd been then. Perhaps it was all the chat I'd been giving him.

Being so cheerful was wearing me out, so gradually I let the one-sided conversation slide. I went to my room for a while, but I couldn't stay up there, I had to get him to notice me. I can't stand being invisible, I think dying must be like that. Being a ghost is like that anyway. You're there, but no one knows you are, and everyone ignores you.

I went downstairs again. He was in the kitchen with Ella and Jude, but he wasn't saying much to them either. He had his head in his hands and he seemed very still. I went and stood beside him, and I said, 'The fireworks yesterday were very good. I liked the red ones best.' Ella gave me a warning look, but I didn't see why I should take any notice of her. 'I also liked the yellow ones,' I said, still sounding bright. It's hard, thinking of things to say when no one's talking back, so I asked him, 'Have all the mice gone yet?' It was mean of me to remind him about the mice because he hadn't done anything about them, he kept saying he'd see to it tomorrow. I felt like getting at him though. You do feel like that when someone isn't talking to you.

It got a flicker from him. He raised his head and looked at me angrily. I decided that this was the right approach. If I could get him really mad, he might say something to me.

'I haven't tidied my room, it's a pit. It is *my* room

though. If I want it to be a mess, I don't see why I shouldn't be allowed to.'

Ella came over to the table and said in a low voice, 'Shut up, Bessie. What do you think you're doing?'

'Talking,' I said meaningfully.

'Leave it.'

She took me by the arm but I shrugged her off and stood closer to Dad, so that I was right beside his chair and our shoulders were touching. Dad looked at me again and said, 'Why are you doing this?'

I nearly didn't answer, I thought I might give him a taste of his own medicine, but it didn't seem right not to reply, so I said, 'Doing what?'

'Behaving like this. Being so rude all the time.'

'I'm not.'

'If she was here, your mother would be ashamed of you.'

He always did that. He always mentioned Mum when I was least expecting it and made me want to cry. It was his worst tactic.

Jude said, 'I want a biscuit.' This was her only answer to family quarrels. She'd grow up fat as a pig.

Dad repeated his question to me. 'I asked you why you're behaving like this. Does it give you pleasure to make us all miserable?'

'You don't mind making me miserable. Anyway, I wasn't, I was being bright and cheerful.'

Dad suddenly stood up. His hand shot out and he caught the side of my head. I stumbled back into a chair. Ella stood half-way between us, not knowing what to do. I looked at Dad in disbelief. He'd never, ever, hit me before. I put my hand to my head and felt tears behind my eyes but I was determined not to let them fall.

'I hate you,' I said, but I didn't say it with the usual temper, I said it as if I meant it. My head stung and its smarting made me stop caring about what could happen next. 'I wish Mum was here now as well because she'd be ashamed of *you* too. And if you want to know why I behave like I do, it's because she would be here if it wasn't for you and your stupid moods. It was your fault she got in that accident, it was all because of you, and I hate you, I wish you'd died instead and I'm never ever going to forgive you for it.'

My legs were shaking. It *was* his fault, all of this, it was, and he deserved to be told about it. So why, as I looked at him, did I feel so sad and mean? Why did it feel so wrong to have told the truth? No one in our house told the truth, not him and not Ella. Jude did sometimes, but only because she was six and didn't know any better.

There was silence again. It was a worse sort of silence than the one there'd been when he wasn't talking to me. It was the kind of silence that tells you that something very bad is about to happen. I waited. Then Dad said, 'You're right, it was my fault. I am to blame, I know that.'

Ella said, 'It was no one's fault, Dad, it wasn't, it was just an accident.'

He didn't reply.

Jude tried to put her arms around him but he pushed her away, not roughly, but she knew he didn't want her and she started to cry.

He looked at her, and then he looked at me, and then he looked at Ella. 'It's no use, is it?' he said.

'What do you mean? What's no use?' Ella asked.

He did't answer her.

Ella said, 'Go upstairs and play, Jude, I'll come up in a minute.' She didn't move, so Ella added, 'Go on, darling, do what you're told. I'll come up and read to you if you like.'

Jude got up reluctantly.

I knew why Ella had sent her up. She was afraid of what was going to happen too. Dad was over by the sink, staring out across the tiny back yard. Gary was opposite again, I could see him. He was kicking a ball against the wall over and over. It thudded against the brick and sent up clouds of dust. I went and stood next to Dad. I wanted to hug him the way Jude had wanted to, but I was afraid he'd push me away too. Why had I said all that stuff about Mum? I wanted to tell him I was sorry but the words wouldn't come out.

'Dad,' said Ella.

He half turned towards her. 'What is it?'

'Bessie didn't mean it. She doesn't really believe what she said, do you?'

I shook my head, but Dad wasn't looking at me, he was looking out of the window again.

We stood there for the longest time. Then suddenly Dad said, 'I'm going out.'

I was relieved. If we were going somewhere, he

couldn't be feeling too bad about what I said, he couldn't be taking it to heart.

'I'll get Jude ready,' said Ella.

'No, you're staying here.'

Ella and I looked at each other uncertainly. 'Can't we come with you?' Ella said.

'I need time on my own, I have to have some quiet. I need to think about things.'

'We'll be quiet, Dad, really we will, I promise,' said Ella, but he went upstairs as if he hadn't heard her.

We followed him into his room. Jude was there. She'd found a pair of Mum's high-heeled shoes and was tottering around in them. I was worried that this would upset Dad, but he didn't say anything.

'I'm going to be a mother and buy a pair of high heels when I get some money,' said Jude.

'You'll never get that much money,' I answered, but I didn't get through to her, she went on to describe exactly what the shoes would look like.

Dad was putting on a shirt, but he was doing the buttons up wrong, the way Jude would. I wanted to tell him but I didn't like to, I'd said enough already. Why had I done it? He looked more unhappy than I had ever seen him. I wanted to tell him Ella was right, I was sorry, it wasn't his fault, I knew he hadn't caused the accident, but my head still hurt and also, I was scared. I wished he wasn't going out though. Didn't he know he hadn't shaved yet? He put on a pair of trainers and a hooded top that had shrunk in the wash and looked a size too small. Then he went downstairs again.

'Can't we all go?' asked Ella again.

'I won't be long,' said Dad, ignoring the question.

'You can't go, it's –' I saw Dad's face and stopped. He looked as if he was going to cry. Grown-ups don't cry unless somebody dies. Fathers don't cry even then.

He opened the front door. 'Dad, I'm sorry,' I said, but I don't know if he heard me. He went out, closing the door behind him.

I went into the kitchen. There, on the table, was Dad's wallet and the keys to the house. I picked them up and ran out into the street, but there was no sign of him. He'd already disappeared out of sight.

Eleven

I was in the living-room trying to read, but I could barely see the page in front of me. It was getting dark but I didn't want to switch on the light. I think I was trying to hold off the end of the day by pretending it wasn't happening. I drew a deep breath and looked at the clock on the mantelpiece. Almost seven. It was earlier than I had expected, but still, Dad should have been back hours ago. A terrible fear began to grow. What if he'd had an accident, like Mum? What would we do? I began to read again with even greater speed and concentration. That was why I liked reading, it helped to shut out all the bad thoughts about what could happen in the future.

The sound of Jude's footsteps dragged me back into the real world. She switched on the light, and it threw out a harsh glare that made me rub my eyes. 'What do you want?' I said.

'Nothing,' replied Jude. 'I just thought I'd come and sit with you because Ella's so *verminous*.'

Jude liked that word too. She used it at every opportunity. 'What's Ella been doing then?' I asked. I was curious. I was mean to Jude all the time, but Ella hardly ever was.

'She told me to get lost. She said our room was

mainly hers. She said she'd slap me if I didn't get out.'

It seemed to me that Jude was enjoying the role of wronged little sister even more than usual, so I wasn't going to encourage her. 'I expect you asked for it,' I said.

'I'll tell Dad when he gets home, and he'll be cross with Ella. He'll be cross with you too.'

Normally, I didn't let Jude get away with threats, but I was too busy wondering when Dad was coming back to bother sorting her out.

'I want Dad,' said Jude, her voice rising to a whine.

I swallowed my irritation and replied, 'Come and sit here and don't be a baby.' I pulled her on to the sofa beside me.

'When's Dad coming home?'

My insides tumbled as I thought of the possible answers. 'Soon,' was all I said.

'Ella's crying. Is it because Dad isn't back yet?'

I shrugged, and wished I could get on with my book instead of being faced with Jude's impossible questions. Ella had had the right idea, sending her downstairs to plague me instead.

'Why isn't he back now?'

'Maybe he met a friend.'

'Has something happened to him?'

'No, it hasn't.'

'How do you know?'

'I just do. I tell you what, I could read you a story.'

'I don't want a story,' said Jude with an impatient wriggle. 'I want to watch television.'

'It's all grown-up stuff now.'

'I don't care, I've watched war things and everything. I saw a bit of *Terminator 2*. I wasn't scared.'

'When was that?'

'When I was staying with my friend Robert and we lived at the old house.'

'I bet Dad never knew you saw that. He'd have killed you. He wouldn't even let me watch that.'

Jude looked pleased as Punch that she'd managed to see something I hadn't.

'You should be in bed,' I reminded her. 'When Dad comes home, you'll be in trouble for being up so late.'

'He won't mind if I wait up for him. You can tell me a story if you want.'

'How very kind of you to let me,' I said with heavy sarcasm, but it was lost on Jude.

'I don't want a real story, I only like pretend ones. They're more interesting.'

'What did you think I was going to give you? The Nine o'Clock News?'

Jude looked blank, so I said, 'I don't think I want to tell you a story any more. You've lost your chance.'

'Oh go on, I'll be good.'

'You wouldn't know how,' I told her, but I took a book off the shelf and began reading one of the stories. It was called *The Three Little Pigs*.

'Is the wolf going to eat them?' asked Jude, after a page or two.

'Wait and see,' I said sternly. I was better at this story stuff than I'd expected. I quite liked reading aloud, I could do all the different voices and really make it come alive.

I must have been livening it up a bit too much for Jude because she said, 'It must be terrible to be a little pig and have the wolf waiting to eat you all the time.'

'It's only a story. It isn't real. You said you didn't want a real one.'

'It feels real though.'

Jude was right, it did feel real. Although I was quite enjoying the reading, it was getting to me too. I knew how those little pigs felt, waiting for something terrible to happen all the time. 'I'll huff and I'll puff and I'll blow your house down.' It was as if the wolf had visited us already and had blown one house down so that Mum had had the accident and we'd had to move. What if more bad things were happening? What if Dad wasn't coming home any more?

'It isn't real though,' said Jude, as the wolf uttered more terrible threats.

'No, it isn't real,' I repeated, as much for my own sake as for Jude's. 'Anyway, the pigs are all right in the end, they build themselves a proper house that the wolf can't blow down and they all live happily ever after.'

'You've spoilt it now,' said Jude, with a wail. 'It's no good going on with it now I know the ending.'

I closed the book.

'But you can read it to me anyway,' she added generously. 'You could have remembered it wrong. Ella says you don't remember things properly. She says it's because you don't bother to listen.'

'Ella can go stick her head in a bucket,' I replied crossly. I opened the book again. I was getting sleepy now. Jude was too; her eyes were closing. The clock said five to eight. What was Ella doing? She should have been putting Jude to bed. I decided to take her up myself once I'd finished the pig story and then maybe I'd be able to get on with my own book. I wondered where Dad had got to. It was mean of him to stay out so long and worry us. It wasn't fair. He was a grown-up; he ought to have known better.

Someone was shaking me. 'Dad?' I said.

'No, it's me.'

I looked at Ella sleepily. I was still in the chair, with Jude snoring like a piglet beside me.

'Don't wake her,' said Ella, 'she'll only bawl.'

Even in the dim light, I could see that Ella had been bawling herself. 'Isn't Dad home yet?' I asked, though I knew the answer, it was there in Ella's face. 'What time is it?'

'One o'clock.'

'In the morning?'

'It's pitch dark, so it must be one o'clock in the afternoon, mustn't it?'

I remembered what Jude had said about Ella being mean to her. She wasn't usually the sarcastic type, she left that to me and Dad. 'Where do you think he's got to?' I asked Ella, after a moment or two of silence. I wasn't sure I wanted to have my fears confirmed, but at the same time, it was stupid to pretend it wasn't happening.

Ella sat beside me on the sofa. 'I don't know,' she said in a tight voice.

'Do you think we should phone someone?' I asked.

Jude stirred. Ella froze and put her finger to her lips to hush me for a moment. I knew what she meant. If Jude woke up at this hour and Dad wasn't there, we'd have to spend all our time calming her down.

Jude started breathing evenly again, so Ella answered, 'Who can we phone?'

'The police. Hospitals. That's what people do in books.'

Ella shook her head.

'Why not?'

'Because we're here on our own.'

'Of course we're here on our own. That's the point. That's why we ought to be phoning someone,' I said impatiently. Ella was so slow.

'He shouldn't have left us. Bess, it was on television. A mother nearly got sent to prison for leaving her kids by themselves late at night.'

'Yes, but they were young kids. I'm eleven. You're thirteen.'

'It's still not allowed. They'd say he was a bad parent and they'd take us away from him.'

I wondered who Ella meant when she talked

about 'they'. I had an image of rough-looking men in long dark coats who arrested children in the middle of the night because of the things their parents had done. 'Is "they" the police?'

'It's social workers, people like that.'

'What can we do then?'

'We can't do anything, that's what I'm saying.'

I was silent for a moment, trying to work out what would happen if we did something, and what might happen if we didn't. 'So we can't tell anyone that Dad hasn't come home?' I said at last.

'That's what I'm telling you,' said Ella. 'Why don't you listen? Anyway, he could come back any minute. There are lots of reasons for being late, it doesn't always mean something's gone wrong, and it doesn't mean he isn't coming back at all. It could be anything, it's stupid to worry, just stupid!'

I suddenly wanted to hug Ella the way I was hugging Jude. I wanted us all to be snug and safe against the wolf. I just sat there though. Then, after a while, I said, 'I think we should go to bed. When Dad comes home, he'll want to know what we're doing up so late.'

'I don't know if we can do it without waking Jude.'

'I should think we can,' I said. 'Mum always managed it. We could both carry her. Ella, could I sleep in your bed, at the end, just for tonight? It would be better, wouldn't it?'

Ella nodded. 'Help me lift Jude. It's easier with two of us.'

'I know,' I said, but Jude was heavy and it was

a struggle to get her up the stairs. More than once she stirred, but she didn't wake up, not even when we pulled off her dress and covered her with blankets. 'It'll be all right, you'll see,' I said to Ella. 'I'm never wrong about these things.'

'Of course you are,' Ella answered, 'you're wrong all the time, it's just that you never see it.'

Any other time, I would have argued with her, but that night it was different. I needed her, I didn't want to think that I was all alone. And besides, she hadn't blamed me for Dad's disappearance, she hadn't said a word about what I'd done. I owed her one for that.

'Aren't you going to get washed?' she asked me.

'No,' I said. 'We don't have to.' It was true. You only have to do things when there are grown-ups around to nag you. I pushed the thought out of my head. If I began to be even the tiniest bit pleased that Dad wasn't home, we might never see him again. It was like putting the evil eye on something, you had to be really, really careful. I burrowed down beside Ella's feet. Once or twice I thought I heard the front door, but when I didn't hear Dad's footsteps on the stairs, I knew I was only dreaming.

Twelve

I woke up feeling stiff. At first I wasn't sure where I was and then I realized I was in Ella's room, squashed at the bottom of the bed. I remembered Dad. I scrambled off the bunk and ran into his room. His bed was empty. I hurried downstairs in case he was in the kitchen, but there was no sign of him. I tried each room in turn with the same result. Dad hadn't come home then. I curled up in the worn armchair in the living-room and began to sob.

It was some minutes before I was able to stop. I sat up straight and felt in my sleeve for a tissue. It was stupid to cry about things, it didn't do any good. When it was over, you just felt tired, and the problems were exactly the same as they'd been before. The practical approach was best, and I was the practical member of the family, everyone said that. So, if I really was as practical as they made out, I ought to pull myself together and start to think about what we should do next.

We couldn't tell anyone that we were on our own, that was the first thing. I realized that Ella had been right about that. If I could work out why Dad hadn't come back, that might help. Maybe he'd had an accident. He could have gone back to

Leeds for some reason, but why would he leave Ella and Jude? I knew why he'd gone away from me, that was obvious, it was because of the things I'd said. I hadn't meant to, I just hadn't been able to stop myself. Everything going wrong so suddenly had made me angry with everybody, even though it was nobody's fault, I knew that now. I suppose I'd always known it. But now I was being punished for saying all that stuff. Dad had gone away.

I went into the kitchen and got myself some biscuits, which I ate at the kitchen table. It was no good getting miserable about what I had or hadn't done, it was better to concentrate on how to get through this. Dad would come back, he had to. It was just a question of holding things together in the meantime. We'd have to be very grown-up and sensible or someone would realize we were by ourselves, and next thing we knew, we'd be in care. The word 'care' conjured up pictures of cell-like rooms and separation. Me and Ella and Jude would all be sent to different places. There'd be foster-homes, most probably, and Dad would come home again and we'd be gone and he wouldn't know where we were and he'd scour the country but never find us again. So if we were going to prevent all that, we had to stop any grown-up finding out that Dad had gone. That was the most important thing.

I took some slices of bread out of the wrapper and put them under the grill. Part of being sensible and grown-up was sharing the chores. Something was going on upstairs. I listened for a moment, but it was only Jude running across the floor. I got out marmalade and Marmite and put them on the table. Then I went to the foot of the stairs. 'Breakfast is ready!' I shouted.

There was a muffled response from Ella that I only half heard. Then Jude hurled herself into the kitchen. 'Where's Dad?' she said.

'Gone out,' I replied.

'He must have come in very late last night,' said Jude. 'I was asleep.'

I didn't answer. Me and Ella would have to decide between us how much Jude should know and we'd have to make sure that she didn't blab our business to every stranger in sight.

Ella wandered in. She looked crumpled and unsure, as if she was barely awake.

'I've done breakfast,' I announced, pleased with myself.

Ella sat down and reached for a cup. 'Is there any milk?' she said.

I went and opened the front door. There was a bottle of milk on the step. I brought it in and put it on the table.

'Thanks,' said Ella. 'He isn't home, is he?'

I shook my head and gestured towards Jude, who was digging her knife into the last scraping of marmalade. Ella understood and fell silent.

'What time is it?' asked Ella after a while.

I didn't know, so I went into the living-room to look at the clock on the mantelpiece. 'Quarter to twelve,' I said as I returned.

'*Quarter to twelve?*' repeated Ella.

'Looks like we overslept,' I said, as calmly as I could. It was obvious that Ella was about to work herself into a panic and we needed to stay sensible. 'Jude, go and get dressed,' I ordered firmly.

'But I haven't finished my breakfast yet.'

'Do what I tell you. Go on, do it now.'

'You can't boss me. Only Dad can tell me what to do.'

'He isn't here right now.'

'Ella then. Dad or Ella are the only people who can make me do things.'

Ella said, 'Finish your breakfast and then go up.'

I felt myself turning pink. Here I was, trying to keep everything running smoothly in spite of all that had happened, and Ella was behaving as if nothing I said even counted. 'You can't . . .' I began, and then stopped. There was no point in arguing, not now. I decided to save it for later, when Dad came home, perhaps.

It was another half-hour before Jude went upstairs. It was as if she knew we wanted to be rid of her. I heard her running the water in the bathroom and knew it was safe to speak. 'What are we going to tell her?' I asked.

'Who?'

'Jude, of course, who do you think?'

'We don't have to tell her anything.'

I turned on the hot water tap and started putting the dirty dishes in the sink. I waited for Ella to comment on how good I was being, but she didn't say a word. I noticed Dad's wallet on the draining board where I'd left it the previous day. 'Dad forgot his wallet. He can't have meant to go far. I mean, where can you go if you don't have any money? He can't have gone back to Leeds.'

'I guess not,' said Ella.

'We will have to tell Jude something. She thinks Dad came home last night while she was asleep. I went along with it and told her he'd gone out again this morning.'

'What did you do that for?' asked Ella wearily. 'She's got to know what's happening. She'll find out soon enough.'

'Once she knows, she'll probably tell the first grown-up she sees. You know what she's like.'

'There aren't any grown-ups for her to tell. We're here on our own, don't you realize that?'

Ella put her head on her arms and began to cry. I let her for a while, and then I said, 'There isn't any point in crying, it doesn't help.'

'It helps me,' said Ella in a choky voice, but I didn't understand her. Tears were a waste of energy as far as I was concerned, and we needed our energy for sorting out the mess.

'I hate him!' said Ella suddenly.

I dipped a plate into the suds. The bubbles reflected pink and blue light. It was pretty.

'How could he do this? I hate him, the stinking old –'

I kept my eyes on the bubbles. Ella was practically never angry, she was almost always quiet and kind, and now, here she was shouting about Dad and getting nearly hysterical. 'Don't, Ella,' I said,

120

but it was as if I hadn't said a word, Ella kept on and on saying how much she hated Dad and how he shouldn't have left us. 'Ella, shut up!' I said.

'He doesn't care about us, he doesn't give a damn, he's just walked out –'

'There's a reason, there must be.'

'Like what?' screamed Ella, through her tears. 'Go on, tell me. What reason?'

'He might have had an accident. He might be ill. Anything could have happened, but I bet he hasn't just left us, he wouldn't do it.' I was saying this as much to convince myself as to calm Ella. Jude came in then and I told her to go back upstairs and finish dressing.

'What's the matter?' she said. 'Why are you shouting?'

'Nothing's the matter,' I answered. 'Go back upstairs.'

'Why's Ella crying?' Jude sat at the table beside Ella and put her arms around her. 'Don't cry,' she said.

I put more washing-up liquid in the water and tried to make the bubbles form again, but the colours wouldn't appear. Then I went over to Jude and pulled her gently from the table. I took her upstairs and began to get her dressed.

When I came back down, Ella was quiet and the washing-up was done. It was some time before we spoke. Then Ella said, 'I wish I knew what had happened.'

'Me too,' I answered.

'We have to tell Jude.'

'Yes, but not yet. Dad could walk through the door any minute, you know how he's been, he doesn't always remember the time. He probably doesn't realize how long he's been away. Remember when he told us he had flu? He didn't know how many days he'd been like that. We had to tell him.'

Ella nodded.

'At least we've got money,' I said.

'What do you mean?' asked Ella.

I pointed to the wallet on the draining-board. 'There's some money in there. And then there are the tins for rent and all the other bills. Maybe there's something in them too.'

'We can't touch that.'

'Why not?'

'Because . . .' Ella stopped. Then she said, 'He doesn't care about us. Why should we care about him?' She picked up the wallet. Then she found each of the tins and took them upstairs.

The rest of the day dragged. It was only towards evening when there was still no sign of Dad that I realized how much I'd been counting on him coming home. I'd been sitting downstairs, playing with Jude, listening for the sound of the front gate. Every now and then something would happen; a leaflet would be pushed throught the letter-box or the wind would cause the gate to swing on its hinges and I'd fly into the hall, in the hope that Dad would be there looking like his old self and telling us that everything was going to be all right. When night came and he still hadn't returned, I felt desperate.

We'd told Jude that Dad had gone to meet a friend of his and he'd probably stay the night. Jude had been puzzled but she hadn't asked questions. I suppose that so many strange things had happened lately that one more didn't make much difference.

Ella had been up in her room most of the day. She was hardly talking to me. I knew she was starting to realize how much I was to blame for Dad going off. I didn't want to give her the chance to start yelling at me again, so I put Jude to bed by myself at the usual time and read her a story, while Ella stayed on the top bunk, pretending none of it was happening.

Once Jude had dropped off, we both went downstairs to watch the news. I didn't tell Ella but I had the idea that if anything had happened to Dad it would be on television. Looking back, I suppose it was stupid; loads of people get ill or have accidents every day, and unless they're little kids who need heart transplants or bone marrow donors, they don't come on TV. I guess I wasn't thinking straight.

The news finished without any mention of Dad. I don't know if I was disappointed or relieved.

Ella said, 'It's so quiet, isn't it?' and I nodded, but it didn't seem quiet at all to me, I was aware of every sound the house was making. The noise of the water gurgling through the pipes, the tick of the clock, the rush of wind rattling through the chimney and causing the window-panes to shudder, each of these sounds reminded me that anyone could blow our little house down with the slightest of puffs. I knew I had to believe in happy endings, and that like the three little pigs, we would beat the wolf and send him off with his tail between his legs. But that night, sharing Ella's bed, I dreamt only of piglets and wolves and falling-down houses.

Thirteen

We weren't on the phone, so I knew Dad couldn't ring, but I thought he'd send some sort of message, just to tell us that he was OK. I checked the post next morning, sifting through the bills and circulars, but there was nothing.

It was another late morning. We couldn't seem to get up without Dad, partly because we didn't go to bed till late any more. We were scared of the night so we stayed up for as long as possible, trying to fend it off. We watched night-time television and played Monopoly or snakes and ladders.

I called Jude. It was obvious that Ella had gone to pieces and wasn't playing mother any longer, so it was up to me. Jude came downstairs slowly. She was miserable and lost, and it showed in the way she moved. She didn't hurl herself around any more, she went carefully, as if she was afraid of something. It got on my nerves, but I was trying not to be cross, or at least, I wasn't any crosser than stand-in mothers usually are.

Jude started to cry. It was all I could do not to shout at her, she was such a baby. 'Promise you won't be cross,' she said.

'I won't,' I answered, through clenched teeth.

'I wet the bed.'

I ran upstairs, hoping the wet patch would be a small one. It wasn't. 'You're so stupid,' I told Jude, who was close behind me.

'I'm sorry,' Jude wailed. I could tell she was ashamed of herself, so I stopped shouting at her.

Ella's bed was empty; she was obviously in the bathroom. She was the oldest, she should have been the one who had to worry about this, not me. Trouble was, right then, Ella was useless.

I knew I ought to strip the bed, but there weren't any more clean sheets and the launderette was three streets away. Anyway, I didn't know how to use the machines. I wished I'd paid more attention when we'd gone with Dad. Still, it was too late now, and there was no point in wishing for anything. 'We'll just have to hope it dries,' I said.

Jude nodded.

'We'll put it over the banisters and then it'll dry quicker.' I pulled the sheet off the bed and draped it over the wooden banisters that lined the landing. Then I went downstairs to get some breakfast.

The day before, we'd found a pound coin down the side of the sofa. We'd used it to buy a giant Swiss roll from the supermarket. We'd decided to have it for breakfast because cake at breakfast time wasn't allowed when the grown-ups were around. I cut my hunk and quite enjoyed it. The idea of doing something that was normally forbidden was exciting. There were probably quite a few things we could do now that no one had let us do before. I tried to think of some but my mind was a blank. Typical. It's always hard to remember forbidden pleasures when they stop being forbidden any more. The shine goes out of them.

Ella came down. She still wasn't dressed, though she smelled of soap, which was a relief. Yesterday, she'd taken a leaf out of Dad's book and hadn't even combed her hair.

'Jude wet the bed,' I told her.

'I know,' said Ella.

'I put the sheet over the banisters to let it dry. It should be ready again by tonight.'

'You washed it?'

'No, of course not, it's too big.'

'Then it'll stink the place out.'

'You do it then,' I said angrily. Who did Ella think she was? She bossed us all the time when Dad was around and she didn't need to, and now, just when some of Ella's bossing would have been quite useful, she'd decided to do next to nothing.

She broke off her portion of the Swiss roll and bit into it. 'It seems funny,' she said.

'It tasted all right to me.'

'No, I mean it seems funny because it's for breakfast. It's too sweet.'

'I liked it,' I said. 'I like doing things I'm not supposed to.'

'You don't say,' answered Ella, with unusual sarcasm. 'You know, if we used the money in the tins and the wallet, we could have cake all the time if we wanted.'

'And ice-cream,' I answered.

'We could get tons of sweets and eat them all at once if we liked.'

'Toffee apples,' I said, thinking of the way the toffee clagged to your teeth so that you had to ease it out with a finger. 'You wouldn't even have to be polite when you were eating,' I said, smiling to myself at the very thought.

Ella flicked a piece of Swiss roll into the far corner of the kitchen. 'I'm not going to pick it up,' she said.

I dropped the cellophane wrapper on the floor. 'Me neither. It would be nice to buy lots of doughnuts.'

'And crisps,' said Ella. She gave me a sideways look. 'I meant what I said about using that money. We have to have something to live on. Who knows when he's coming back?'

I nodded, though I was kind of uneasy about this new, do nothing, devil-may-care Ella that was emerging.

'What did he think we were going to eat while he was gone? Fresh air?' she said.

I glanced out of the window. It was misty. The air looked anything but fresh.

'We have to spend some of it,' Ella said firmly. 'It would serve him right completely if we did.'

This was my kind of logic, but hearing it from Ella was odd. I nodded though. I liked the idea of crisps and all the chocolate I could eat. I could eat myself sick if I wanted to. I cut a thin piece of swiss roll from Jude's share and added it to my own.

I changed into some warmer clothes as quickly as I could. I'd been so miserable, and now I suddenly felt hopeful and excited. We were going to the West End of London to see the big shops where Mum used to take us at Christmas time. We had money, we could do anything we wanted, go anywhere we pleased, and no one could say no to us. I fingered the woollen threads of my worn jumper. Maybe Ella would let me buy a purple sweatshirt. Purple was my favourite colour then and I could just see myself in one. And I wouldn't feel guilty, no, not at all. Ella was right. If Dad wanted us to be good, he shouldn't have left us.

I went into Ella's room, and nearly walked straight out again. Ella was pummelling a pillow with her fists. Then she slung it at the wall and chucked two china ornaments after it. They exploded into fragments. She started to cry. I wasn't sure what to do; she was behaving so strangely. I sat on the floor beside her and put my arm round her, the way Mum used to do with us when we were upset. She twitched as if she was going to shake me off, but then she clutched me in this tight hug that was nearly suffocating. I sat absolutely still, hoping she would stop, and in the end, she did. She crawled to the side of the room and scrubbed her eyes with a tissue that was hard and flaking with all the crying she'd already done.

Jude came and stood over her. 'Are you cross because I wet the bed?' she said.

Ella drew Jude towards her. 'No, it's not you, honest,' she said.

'What is it then?'

'I don't know. It's nothing, really. We're going out.'

'Where are we going?'

'We're going to the shops. Big shops. We're going to buy things.'

'What things?'

'Whatever we want,' Ella replied.

'Can I have ice-cream?' asked Jude.

'You bet,' said Ella.

'You bet,' repeated Jude. 'You bet, you bet, you bet.'

It felt strange, starting out on our own, not having to tell anyone where we were going, not having to ask anyone's permission. I walked on one side, Ella on the other, and Jude skipped along between us. We were holding hands. It felt safer.

'Are we going to get a bus?' asked Jude.

'We're going on the tube,' I said firmly. I'd just decided it that minute. The London underground seemed far more exciting and forbidden than a bus.

We didn't have change for the machine at the station, so we queued at the ticket office. I was put in charge of asking for three child fares to central London because Ella was too nervous; she said her voice would squeak. No one questioned us about being on our own at a busy station in term-time. We were relieved. I'd been scared that it would show in our faces or in the way we walked or dressed or talked that we were alone now. It seemed like such a big secret that it was hard to believe that nobody knew.

We'd just missed a train, so we sat on blue plastic

seats that were joined together in a row. It reminded me of the time we took Jude to the hospital. I thought of Gran, and suddenly it occurred to me that Dad might have gone to see her. That would explain everything, it made absolute sense. I turned to Ella and told her my idea excitedly, but she thought it was silly. 'Gran would never let Dad stay with her if we were on our own,' she said.

My excitement faded. 'Maybe she doesn't realize,' I said, but that didn't seem likely.

'He wouldn't even speak to her at the hospital, so why would he go round to see her?'

Ella was right, it didn't make sense. It was just that I desperately needed to find some explanation for his disappearance, other than the idea that he had gone away from us because of the terrible things I'd said.

When the train came in, we grabbed three vacant seats. I looked at my reflection in the darkened glass window. I couldn't decide if I was pretty or not, but I didn't know if I wanted to be. Pretty was dull. It was better to be exciting – *mad, bad and dangerous to know*. I'd heard the phrase in a film once and I'd thought it described me absolutely. I wasn't a safe person, like Ella, I was moody and rebellious, which was a lot more interesting. I glanced at her. She certainly was pretty, though she didn't seem to know she was, she didn't see that Carl obviously thought she was very pretty indeed. But then, that was just like Ella, she didn't notice anything much. It was probably very boring, being Ella; she was so nice. Then I remembered that Ella hadn't been very nice at all since Dad had gone. She'd been in a sulk and she hadn't done much round the house. I also remembered the way she'd thrown Swiss roll on the floor. And spending the money had been Ella's suggestion, not mine, I hadn't even thought about it.

Well, maybe that wasn't strictly true. I had thought about it, but I hadn't wanted to do it, in case in some mysterious way it stopped Dad coming back. I still felt a bit funny about doing something I knew he wouldn't like, which was odd really, because I disobeyed all the time, I was always getting into trouble. It was different when grown-ups were actually around though. You couldn't just do everything you were told or they'd think they could order you about as much as they wanted. You had to break the rules, that's what they were there for. But once the grown-ups had gone, there weren't any rules, and that was kind of scary.

The train stopped at Oxford Circus. For a moment, it didn't look as if we'd manage to get out. There were so many people squashed against the door that it was blocked and nobody could move. Ella shouted, 'Let me out!' in a panicky voice, and slowly, the crush began to ease enough for us to shove our way through. We stood on the busy platform. Ella still looked shaky and scared. She whispered to me that she didn't like the underground, and said she'd heard that there were rats that came out at night when everything was quiet. I'm a far cooler and more adventurous person than Ella, but I wasn't so sure about this place either. It was gloomy and stuffy, yet there was also a draught from one of the tunnels that seemed to propel you along every now and then. I wondered what it would be like to be there alone in the darkness, deep underground, stuck down there for ever. It made me think of Dad, stuck somewhere – he had to be, or he'd have come home.

I said, 'Hurry up, Ella, it's boring down here,' and she quickened her steps and followed me and Jude up the escalators towards daylight.

Oxford Circus was crazy. Ella said it was all her worst crowd nightmares rolled into one, but I thought it was one of the most exciting places I'd ever been to. There were two kinds of people; those who scurried along, barging their way through, and those who meandered so that you trod on their heels when you tried to take a step. Ella was a meanderer, but I was definitely a barger. When Mum was young, they'd had this type of dancing called slam dancing, where you had to crash into other people on the dance floor. Oxford Circus was full of slam dancers and I joined them. 'It's dangerous, isn't it?' I said to Ella, relishing every moment.

Ella said, 'Dad was right, London isn't safe, anything could happen here, we could be murdered even.'

Trust Ella to exaggerate. I had no intention of being murdered, I was having too much fun.

'There's a sign that says Hamleys,' said Jude, pointing along the street.

'It's good that you read that, Jude,' said Ella, in

133

the kind of voice Mum used to use. I wanted to puke.

We arrived outside Hamleys and looked at the window displays. There was a large polar bear, dressed like Santa Claus, skating on ice. It was a bit childish for me.

We went inside, awed by the hugeness of the place.

'Do they only sell toys here?' asked Jude.

'I think so,' replied Ella.

'Truly remarkable,' said Jude solemnly. Ella and I laughed and she got cross and said, 'I didn't say it wrong, I didn't!'

'I know you didn't,' I said. 'It just sounded funny because it was so grown-up.'

Jude liked the idea that she was being adult. She went to look at the display of soft toys with a pleased expression on her face. There were pink pigs with cute faces and open mouths, stuffed to the seams. '*I'll huff and I'll puff . . .*' I thought, but I decided to put that nasty pig story out of my head for now and just enjoy being out. I turned my attention to the purple velvet dinosaurs that Jude was admiring. Then she picked up a shaggy black bear on all fours. It had a kind face. It was so large that she almost disappeared from view. She staggered with the weight. 'I want this,' she said.

'OK,' said Ella. We'd decided that we could each have one thing we really wanted, to stop us feeling so much like *The Three Little Pigs*, but I pulled Ella's arm. 'She can't have that,' I said.

'She can, it's OK. She'll be better if she has something. She might not wet the bed.'

'We can't afford it. It's more than £200.'

Ella looked at me in astonishment. 'But it's just a kind of teddy bear,' she said.

'That's how much it costs though. Look.' I eased the animal out of Jude's arms and held the price tag out for Ella's inspection. She sighed. She put the bear back on the floor.

'Can't I have it?' asked Jude, in a small voice.

'I really wish you could, but it costs so much money,' I answered.

'We've got the money from the wallet and –'

'Shut up,' hissed Ella.

I took Jude to one side. 'Look, you have to keep quiet about the money,' I whispered to her. 'People might ask us questions. They might think we nicked it.'

'It's our money, you said Dad left it for us for food and things.'

'Sort of he did, but it's complicated.' I was starting to realize just how complicated it was, having to think about money and what you were going to live on. An hour ago, it had seemed like so much money, the kind of money you could buy the world with, but now it seemed puny, hardly worth anything at all. How long would it last even if we just bought food, and what would happen if Dad didn't come back before all the money was spent?

Ella came over with a small bear in her hand. 'You could have this one, Jude. Look at him. He's so cute.'

Jude wasn't impressed. 'No, I want that one,' she said. 'I even know his name. He's called Norman.'

'Well,' Ella said, 'Norman's got to stay here with the other bears. He's telling me he'd rather be with his friends.'

'He isn't, he's telling me he wants to come with us. Why can't you hear him properly?'

'Yes, why can't you, Ella?' I said nastily. I was fed up with this already. Now Jude was going to bawl and it was all Ella's fault, she shouldn't have made so many promises about what we could buy with the money.

We prised Jude away from the soft toys and bought her a chocolate ice-cream by way of consolation, but she only took one lick and said she didn't want it. I suppose what she really wanted, what we all really wanted, was for Dad to come back home, and with every moment that passed, it was looking more as if we'd be on our own for ever and ever. I smudged away a tear and hoped no one had seen. Then I said, 'I'm going to buy some bubblegum after this and stick it all over everywhere and no one will be able to tell me off.' I turned away from the other two and watched all the people milling by. Maybe Dad was in the crowd. Maybe we'd see him if we watched very carefully and tried to be good.

If someone had told me that it was possible to go to Oxford Street with money to spend but end up having a miserable time, I wouldn't have believed them, but nothing went right from then on.

I found my purple sweatshirt. It was the right style, right shade, right fit, but for some reason I couldn't actually bring myself to buy it. I suppose I was scared that we'd lose Dad for ever if I did, and fear made me cross and not even burgers in McDonalds made a difference.

Jude was still creating about the bear she didn't get. 'It was so cute,' she kept saying. 'Shut up and stop whinging,' I told her, but you know what little kids are like, they just go on and on.

It was hard, pushing through the crowds with an irritating brat in tow, but we didn't have a choice. There was a shop in a turning off Regent Street that sold cheap toys. Jude chose a spider to make up for the missing bear. I think she did it to spite me. Even toy spiders give me the creeps. Like me, Ella seemed to have lost heart in the spending spree. She didn't show interest in anything.

We were all tired, so we decided to get on a bus to see the sights. Even though it was only November, the Christmas lights were on. It was fir trees with presents hanging from them that year, and they flashed and twinkled in the dusk. They made me think of Mum, so I had to shut them out. I chewed some bubblegum and smeared it on the back of the seat in front.

Ella said, 'Stop it, Bessie,' and gave me a disapproving look.

I didn't care. 'You're not in charge of me,' I said and she shut up again.

We got off at Leicester Square. It was starting to get dark. The smell of frying onions on hot-dog stands made my eyes smart, but it was a smell I liked. I wanted to go to the London Dungeon. I didn't know where it was, but I thought it must be near. Ella said we couldn't because of Jude; it would give her nightmares and she'd probably wet the bed again.

'Jude always spoils things, she's such a baby,' I said.

We walked on in frosty silence. Then, after a while, Ella said, 'Let's be friends.' I knew she couldn't handle quarrels, not in a strange place with everything upside down, because I felt like that too, only I hadn't wanted to be the first to make it up.

'Where to now?' said Ella.

'I don't know,' I answered. We were all tired, but we didn't want to go home to an empty house.

There was a busker a little way ahead, playing a mouth organ and a set of drums and controlling a dancing puppet, all at the same time. We stopped to watch and clapped when he'd finished. He had a hat on the ground in front of him, so Ella and I went to put a few pennies in. It was then that we realized that Jude had gone.

I could feel my heart banging as I looked into the crowd and tried to pick her out. There was no sign. Ella began running back and forth like a mad thing, and I was afraid I'd lose her too. 'Stay with me,' I told her firmly. I took her hand and we weaved in and out of the crowd, looking for Jude's bright green coat. It felt unreal. One minute, she'd been standing beside us, and in the next, she'd gone.

'Maybe she's with Dad,' I said, though I don't know why I thought it possible. We retraced our steps so that we were standing in front of the man with the puppet again. 'We have to stay calm,' I kept saying; it was a phrase Mum used to use in a crisis.

I don't know how long we stood there, wondering what to do. We couldn't go to the police because of Dad. If we couldn't tell anyone what had happened, how would we find her?

'Didn't you see anything?' Ella demanded. 'This is your fault.'

'How can it be because of me?'

'Because you're so horrible,' said Ella. I was so scared and worried, I·almost believed her. And then, suddenly, I saw Jude, holding the hand of a man who sort of looked like Dad but at the same time didn't, he was older and too tall and he was wearing a suit. I ran towards her. 'Jude!' I shouted. She looked at me. She seemed scared. I thought of all the kidnapping stories I'd read in the paper and heard on the news. The man tried to hurry Jude along with him, but she stood stock still and he couldn't drag her. Then suddenly, he let go of her and disappeared into the crowd.

I went up to Jude and grabbed her hand. I started shouting at her. 'You stupid little idiot!' I yelled. 'Why didn't you stay with us?'

'I wanted to see the merry-go-round with the lights on it,' Jude said, pointing ahead to Leicester Square Gardens. A miniature fair was in full swing. 'The man said he'd take me on a ride.'

'You know you must never go with strangers,' said Ella. She sounded as if she was going to cry. 'What would have happened if we hadn't found you?'

'I'd have been all right,' said Jude. 'He was a nice man.'

'He would have taken you away from us and done terrible things to you,' said Ella. She *was* crying now.

'What terrible things?' asked Jude.

We couldn't tell her because we didn't really know, but they were nameless and unthinkable things, to do with being hurt and even dying.

'We have to go home,' said Ella.

I knew that no matter how long we stayed, the day wouldn't get any better, so I followed Jude and Ella, not wanting to go home but not wanting to stay either. Nowhere was safe. Paper sellers on corners called out headlines in strange voices that I could barely understand. I looked at one paper as it lay face up on a news-stand, but there was no mention of Dad. I don't know why I'd thought there would be.

Once on the tube train, we dozed every now and then, though Ella and I kept forcing ourselves awake in case the man who'd wanted to take Jude was still near by.

Jude woke up and got out her rubber spider. It only had six legs. She dangled it in front of me, obviously hoping that I'd show a bit of terror. 'Do you really think I don't know the difference between a stupid rubber spider and a real one?' I said crossly. 'Anyway, it's silly, everyone knows a spider's got eight legs, not six.'

'It was probably a mistake,' said Ella.

'They were all like that, I checked. Perhaps that's why they were cheap,' I answered.

'I think six legs makes him better than ordinary spiders,' said Jude. 'Anyone can be an ordinary spider, but having six legs is special.'

As we walked from the station, I realized how late it must be. It was really dark now, and people were looking at us as if they thought we shouldn't be out on our own at that time of night. We walked quickly. Then up ahead we saw Gary with two bigger boys beside him. He turned round and saw us. 'It's the monkey kids,' he said. 'Shouldn't you be tucked up in bed?' He picked up a stone and flung it into the air. It skimmed past Ella and landed just in front of us. We broke into a run. I looked back and saw that the boys were just standing there, laughing at us. 'Dad's probably home,' I said breathlessly, as we reached our street. We raced to the front door, but as soon as we arrived, we knew there was no one there. The house was still dark. The curtains weren't drawn and there was an emptiness about it that I can't explain.

Ella was in charge of the key, so she let us all in. It was cold inside. We drew the curtains quickly and turned on every light. The house wasn't so creepy when it was brightly lit. There were no shadows then, and fewer dark corners for bogies to hide in.

Fourteen

We began to lose count of the days. Sometimes we could tell whether it was Tuesday or Wednesday by what was on television, but mostly we weren't sure. Then Ella had the idea that we could go to the newsagent and check the day by looking at a paper. If we hurried in and out, we wouldn't even have to buy anything.

Already, we'd spent a lot. Food for three people every single day cost quite a bit, and there were other expenses too, like toilet rolls and washing-up liquid. I'd been seeing the milk that arrived on the doorstep each morning as a free gift, but Ella said the milkman would be round soon and expect us to settle up, so we weren't to open the door to him, or to anybody else for that matter. I said, 'What if it's Dad? He doesn't have his keys,' and Ella replied that we'd have to look out of the downstairs window, but very carefully, so that no one would guess there was anyone home.

It seemed best to go out as little as possible. Some areas had truancy patrols, and kids hanging round shops or stations in term-time were picked up. We had to be very careful, Ella said. I was glad she was thinking about what we should do a bit more, but I'm really not a careful person, careful's dull and boring.

I hated having to stay in the house all the time. For one thing, it was starting to smell. Jude kept wetting the bed and we couldn't keep up with the amount of sheet washing that was needed. We should have emptied the rubbish bin in the kitchen, but somehow, it never got done. And there were piles of washing-up in the sink because I'd got fed up with doing it on my own and Ella was still on early retirement.

I couldn't sit indoors any more, it was doing my head in. So I told Ella I was going out.

'Not by yourself,' she said.

'Why not?'

'Because I don't know if you'll be coming back.'

I could see why this might be a worry. People had been going out and not coming back rather a lot lately. And then there was what had happened to Jude in Leicester Square. So instead of telling Ella not to be stupid, I sat down again and tried to get interested in a Ren and Stimpy cartoon.

The doorbell rang. We froze for a moment, and then I ran into the front room and looked out from behind the curtains. 'It's only Carl and Shirley,' I said, and went to let them in.

'No!' Ella said, but it was too late, I'd already opened the door.

Ella said coldly, 'We can't see you today, our Dad's ill. If you stay, you might wake him.' She gave me a meaningful look.

I understood what was required of me, but I thought Ella was being over-cautious. 'Yes, Dad's ill,' I said. Then, because I didn't see why Ella should decide things, I added, 'But I don't see why you can't stay if you don't make any noise.'

'No!' said Ella again. Carl and Shirley looked at each other in surprise, and I realized that this was only making them suspicious. Ella must have realized this too, because after a moment she agreed that they could come in if they were quiet.

'But there's lots of noise upstairs,' said Shirley.

We listened. We hadn't been aware of it before, but Jude was banging a drum, and blowing on a mouth organ every now and again for emphasis. I ran up. 'You have to be quiet,' I said. 'Shirley and Carl are here. Ella's told them Dad's ill and they mustn't make a noise, and here you are banging on a drum.'

'But Dad's not here,' said Jude, failing, as usual, to get the point.

'I know he isn't. It's what I've told you before, if anyone finds out we're by ourselves without any grown-ups, they'll put us in a children's home and maybe we won't ever see him again.'

Jude looked so horror-struck at this idea that I hastily tried to take it back. 'It's not going to happen because nobody will find out, will they? You're not going to tell, and I'm not going to tell, and Ella isn't going to tell either. You don't have to worry as long as you're careful.'

Jude nodded. 'When is Dad coming back?' she said.

'Soon,' I told her, 'very soon.'

Jude followed me downstairs. Carl was saying, 'I wish you had some computer games. Tell you what, you could come round to our place again. There's more to do.'

Ella eagerly agreed, but I resented Carl's suggestion that our place was boring. 'I might not want to go,' I told him.

Shirley said, 'Suit yourself,' in a huffy voice so I said quickly, 'But actually, I do want to,' and I began to put on my jacket. Shirley looked at Jude and whispered to me, 'Does she have to come?'

Jude obviously heard because she screwed her face up and opened her mouth to bawl, so Ella said 'Yes,' in a very firm voice before any sound came out. Jude's mouth closed again.

Shirley shrugged but she didn't argue. 'Come on,' was all she said.

As we were following them out, Ella obviously remembered that we ought to pretend that Dad was upstairs. She went up as if to tell him we were going out and called goodbye as we closed the front door.

There was a short cut to Carl and Shirley's place which involved passing Gary's yard. He was lurking by the bins, which seemed the right place for him. As we passed, he called out, 'Get back on your jam-jar,' but we ignored it, walking by with our heads in the air like he was nothing. I suddenly had this awful feeling that he'd find out we were alone. He'd grass us up for sure. I quickened my pace and the others did the same until he was out of sight.

I'd hoped that Carl and Shirley's mum and dad would be out, but they were in the kitchen drinking coffee. We helped ourselves to orange juice and Carl asked if he could make some sandwiches. They had beef and chicken in the fridge. I drooled. I couldn't wait to get my teeth into a chicken drumstick.

We forgot that we were meant to be well brought up and we fell on the plate of food that Carl and Shirley had prepared as if we were half starved. In a way, I suppose we were; we'd eaten too many Swiss rolls and not enough proper food. Shirley's parents raised their eyebrows and asked if we'd had breakfast. That brought us up sharp. Ella began to insist that we had, but Carl broke in and explained that Dad was ill, and his mum and dad looked less surprised at our behaviour then. I tried not to go for third or fourth helpings, but I couldn't stop myself. I realized it was days since we'd eaten anything substantial. I decided to persuade Ella to let us have fish and chips that evening. Sweets were all very well, but you needed to have other things too in order to appreciate them.

Carl took Ella into the sitting-room so that they could watch videos. I didn't know what they wanted to see, but I guessed it would be some lovesick, mushy stuff. I hadn't thought about it up until then, but Ella was probably old enough to go out with boys. It made me feel young and left out. I was huffy for a bit. Then Shirley said, 'What's biting you?' so I gave her some story about Ella being mean to me at home, which was only half true, so then I felt guilty about it.

Jude was lining up Shirley's soft toys in rows and

talking to them all as if she was a teacher. The bear must have been a bear with attitude because she was pounding it and telling it to be good in future. I don't think Shirley was too happy about that, though she didn't stop Jude, which was kind of her really.

'Do you know what school you'll be going to yet?' she asked.

'Dad hasn't decided,' I answered.

'He's a bit slack about things, isn't he?'

'What things?'

'Oh, you know, school, giving you proper meals . . . all that. Wish my mum and dad were a bit slacker. They nag us morning, noon and night.'

'You don't wish that, you know.'

'What do you mean?' asked Shirley, but I wouldn't tell her. After a pause, she added, 'Do you want any more to eat?' I did, but I wasn't sure if I should admit it. Jude didn't hesitate though. 'Can I have some more of that chicken?' she said.

So we ate some more and then played a game of dominoes, which we let Jude win because she was the youngest. Ella and Carl came in and played too and then we went and watched a video about this kid who's left at home by himself and has the best fun ever. It seemed more than coincidence that of all the videos in all the world we should have to watch that one. Ella went very quiet. I quite enjoyed it though. At least it had a happy ending. Jude said, 'That was just like –' but Ella and I jumped in quick before she could continue and said it was time to go home.

'I'll walk you back,' said Carl.

'You don't have to,' I told him, 'it's only round the corner.' And then I realized that what he actually wanted to do was to walk Ella home, the way boys walk girls home in films. I almost puked.

Ella smirked and looked so pleased, it was as if he was giving her an engagement ring. I didn't fancy playing gooseberry all the way home, so I asked Shirley to come with us too. So of course, we all ended up going, which was silly.

We reached the front door and Ella felt in her pocket for the keys. She turned red, and then white. 'I left them indoors,' she said.

'You stupid . . .' I began and then stopped. There was no point in blaming Ella. I could have remembered to check that we had them, but I didn't.

Carl said, 'Your dad'll let you in, won't he?'

Jude said, 'He's not –' but Ella kicked her foot so she shut up.

I rang the bell. I knew, of course, that there wouldn't be any answer, but I thought that if I pretended and waited, Shirley and Carl would go. They remained where they were, though, and we all stood on the doorstep waiting for something that couldn't possibly happen. Then I said, 'He must have gone out.'

'Isn't he ill?' said Shirley.

'He must have been feeling better,' I mumbled.

There was a long silence. Then Carl said, 'There's something going on, isn't there?'

Ella and I said no, but there was just enough hesitation beforehand to confirm it.

'What is it?' asked Shirley in a concerned voice.

'Maybe we can help,' added Carl.

'No one can help,' said Ella, and she sat down on the step looking lost. It was only then that I realized that if we couldn't get inside, everyone would know that we were there alone.

Jude and I sat beside Ella. Jude patted her head. 'Don't be upset,' she said.

Ella looked up. 'I'm not upset, I'm thinking about what to do.'

'Why can't you just wait till your dad gets back?' asked Shirley.

Suddenly I'd had enough of pretending that everything was normal and we were fine. The words just burst out of me. 'Because he's gone away and we don't know where he is. He's been gone for days,' I said.

There was a stunned silence. I was relieved that the pretence was over. Somebody had to say it. Dad might never come home again. There, I'd admitted it to myself. Momentarily, I felt lighter. And then I saw the look of panic on Ella's face and I realized what I'd done. We could all be split up, sent to foster homes like the kids in *Home and Away*, only you could bet there wouldn't be a loving Pippa and Michael to look after us.

Ella said to Carl, 'Please don't tell anyone. *Please.*'

Carl and Shirley sat down beside us on the step. It was a bit of a squash. 'We won't tell anyone,' they said.

Something in their voices made us believe them. Ella looked at Carl, her lost expression gone. 'I've got an excellent idea,' she said.

Fifteen

Ella's plan was obvious; I should have thought of it myself. Because of all the sheet washing we hadn't done, we'd left an upstairs window open. One of us was going to have to climb up the drainpipe, get in through the window and open the front door. All eyes were on me.

'No!' I said.

I'd never told anyone, but I was afraid of heights. At school, I'd always pretended to twist my ankle before rope climbing and I tended to disappear whenever I was expected to enjoy being in a tall building with a view. I'm quite sporty, so no one ever imagines that I'm scared, which is the way I like it. And now, suddenly, I was expected to do a heroic climb up a rickety drainpipe.

Ella said, 'But you must,' in this crushed voice as if she thought I was just being awkward.

I tried defiance. 'No must about it. I'm not going up there and that's that.'

'You never think of anyone but yourself,' said Ella.

'Ditto,' I responded. We glared at one another and then looked up at the window. 'If you're so keen, why don't you do it yourself?' I said.

'But you're the one who can run and jump and all of that,' said Ella.

She was sounding tearful now, and disappointed in me and I couldn't stand her thinking that I didn't care. So I said as casually as I could, 'If you must know, I can't climb up there. I'm scared of heights.' Saying it made me feel stupid. I wanted to run away. Why did Carl and Shirley have to be there? It was bad enough telling Ella and Jude. I looked at the ground. A spider was making its way across the crazy paving. I shuddered. I was just a coward really. It was obvious.

'It's OK,' said Ella kindly.

I wasn't sure I wanted Ella's kindness, but at least she wasn't disappointed in me any more.

'I could do it,' Carl said.

There was a pause. Then Ella said, 'No, this is our problem. I'm going to do it.'

I stared at her. Ella hated gym and games. She never climbed anything. But now, here she was, taking her jacket off and looking determined, like a round-the-world yachtswoman or a climber of Everest.

I suddenly had an image of Ella crashing down from the first-floor window and shattering her skull into a thousand pieces. 'No, you mustn't,' I said. But she walked round to the back of the house, rolling up her sleeves so they wouldn't catch on any foliage.

'Be careful,' said Carl.

I said nothing. I tried to imagine how I would cope if it was just me and Jude. For all her faults, Ella had her uses.

She began the slow climb. Every now and then, she faltered, and I caught my breath. She was half-way up there now, and moving with less hesitation. Maybe she would do it. And then her foot slipped. I cried out, startling her, I think, because she lost concentration and dangled there, unable to find a foothold. 'Move a bit to your right,' Shirley said, but being Ella, she moved left. 'Right!' repeated Shirley, and Ella made the adjustment and found her footing again. She hauled her way, slowly, painfully, to the top, paused for a moment and then pushed the window open enough to let her slide inside. I couldn't help it, I began to clap. We all did. And then suddenly I noticed that Gary was there, peering over the back wall at us, his face alight with curiosity.

'What's going on?' he said.

'Nothing,' I answered. Before he could ask any more questions, Ella opened the front door and we went inside.

The smell of the place hit you as soon as you entered: unwashed sheets, old food, the mustiness I'd been aware of when we'd first moved in. I was embarrassed. Carl and Shirley had that tight look you get when you're trying not to breathe. They followed us silently into the kitchen. There were plates encrusted with age-old baked beans and a crust of bread was turning green in the open bread bin. To add a real touch of sleaze to the picture, a mouse ran from one corner into another so quickly that it was barely visible. Carl and Shirley had seen it though, I could tell by the way their eyes kept returning to the spot.

'Maybe you could use a hand,' said Carl.

'Listen to that,' said Shirley. 'You practically have to beat him up to get him to lend a hand at home.'

Carl ignored this and said, 'It's not hygienic.'

I wanted to tell him to stick his hygiene, but I knew that he was right. I wondered how we could have let the place get into such a state. Ella looked miserable. She must have been wondering what Carl thought of her. Ella always wanted to look good in front of other people in case they stopped liking her. Secretly, I hoped that this would be the end of a beautiful friendship. It wasn't that I wanted a boyfriend myself, I just didn't want Ella to have anything I hadn't got, if that makes sense.

Carl ran the hot tap, but the water was cold. 'I forgot to switch the immersion on,' said Ella in a small voice.

'No problem,' said Carl. 'We'll just have to wait for it to heat up.'

Shirley and I went upstairs. The smell of Jude's sheets was almost overpowering. She was following close behind. She tugged on my sleeve. 'Don't tell Shirley or Gary that I'm dirty,' she whispered.

'You're not dirty,' I whispered back. 'You've just been upset.' I remembered Mum saying once that Jude only wet the bed when she was worried about something. A wave of missing her hit me all of a sudden, but I pushed it away again. I knew we had to be practical if we were going to get through this mess.

Shirley touched the sheets on the banisters warily

with her forefinger and said, 'Someone's wet the bed.'

I just nodded and said that we didn't know how to work the machines in the launderette.

'I know how,' said Shirley. 'Come on, we'll take them now.'

'There's lots of them,' I said. Jude had used up every sheet we had.

'We'll do two today and you can do the other two tomorrow,' replied Shirley decisively. She started to scoop them into her arms and then thought better of it. I can't say I blamed her. Jude and I bundled them into a dustbin bag.

'Does she have to come?' asked Shirley once again, obviously referring to Jude.

'Yes,' I said. It seemed unkind to leave her behind.

We left Ella and Carl clearing up the kitchen and made our way to the launderette. Jude seemed happy and did everything I told her without argument. I think she was relieved that I hadn't shopped her to Shirley over the sheets. The launderette was quiet. Shirley showed me which coins to use and how to put in the soap powder. 'We used to have a washing machine at home in Leeds,' I said, in case she thought we never had clean clothes.

'We've got one now, but when I was little we had to come here,' said Shirley, finding us a seat.

The washing took ages. If Shirley hadn't been there I'd have been bored stupid, but we talked and played I spy and we made up stories, each about what it would be like when we grew up. I left Dad out of all of mine.

Then Shirley said, 'Don't look now, but here comes Gary.'

He stood outside, pressing his nose to the glass and making faces at us. I averted my eyes. Shirley said, 'Let's hope the wind changes,' and we started giggling.

He came inside and said, 'Why did you have to get in through the window then?'

'Because we got locked out. Why do you think?'

'My dad nearly called the cops. He thought it was breaking and entering, but I put him right. He said, "You never know round here. This used to be a nice area until all that lot moved in."'

'In his dreams,' said Shirley.

Gary looked at me and said, 'Don't see you down the club any more.'

'Too busy,' I said. It wasn't that though. Since Dad had gone, we'd had to stay in to look after Jude. It wouldn't have been right to leave her on her own. She'd have been scared.

The washing went into drying mode. I was relieved. I didn't want to hang around there too long with Gary for company.

'Something's going on at yours, isn't it?'

'What do you mean?' I said.

'Something's not right. I can smell it.'

'You couldn't smell bad kippers on a hot day,' said Shirley. We started giggling again.

'I'll find out what's up, you see if I don't. I'm like a bloodhound, me.'

'And just as ugly and flea-ridden,' said Shirley.

'Ugly yourself,' replied Gary. 'You're all just . . .' He couldn't find the words. He stuck his hands in his pockets and mooched outside, whistling as he went.

'You'd better watch him,' said Shirley.

I didn't need telling. If ever there was a mean old wolf, it was that boy Gary.

Ella and Carl were still busy in the kitchen when we returned. It was looking transformed, though. Everything had been washed and wiped dry. Even the grill pan was fat free. Once they'd done the floor, Jude went upstairs to play while we went into the living-room and turned the television on. As the news started, Carl said, 'Where's your dad gone, do you think?'

Ella flashed him a look of fright, and I knew how she felt. The hardest part of all this was not knowing where Dad was. Neither of us answered.

'When do you think he's coming back?' continued Carl.

'I don't know,' said Ella, in a tight voice.

'You mean he's just disappeared?' asked Shirley.

I was tired of the stupid questions. 'That's just what we mean. Leave it, will you?' I said.

But Carl wouldn't drop it. 'Have you tried the police?'

'Don't you understand? If anyone finds out we're here alone, we'll be put into care, so we can't ask anyone where Dad is,' said Ella.

A sudden look of comprehension crossed Carl's face. 'But what are you going to do? You can't stay like this for ever, it's impossible.'

The last thing we needed was common sense, especially when we were trying not to think about the future. 'Who says?' I replied.

'It's obvious, you can't –'

'Shut up,' said Ella.

Carl shut up at once and I was impressed.

'I guess we should be going,' he said, after a long silence. 'We could see you tomorrow or the next day if you want.'

'If you like,' said Ella.

Shirley said, 'If anything happens and you want us, just come round.' I gave her one of my best smiles.

Once they'd gone, I asked Ella what she thought of Carl. 'He's OK,' she said.

'But you like him, don't you?'

'He's OK,' she repeated.

We switched over to an old comedy film that wasn't very funny. I kept laughing though, to hide the worry I was feeling. Then Ella said, 'What do you want to do on your birthday?'

I hadn't thought she'd remember. Just two days to go and I'd be twelve, almost grown-up. Normally, I would have kept on and on about it, but this time there didn't seem to be any point. Mum wouldn't be there. Maybe Dad wouldn't either, but I had this idea that he'd come home then, just so that I'd get a proper present. I was looking forward to it and dreading it at the same time. If he didn't come back that day, he wouldn't be coming back at all, I was certain.

Ella said, 'Come on, Bess, tell me what you want to do.'

'The London Dungeon,' I said. I still hadn't given up on that. I wanted to see the rack, and if there was any blood. But we could only go once Dad was home. We didn't want to miss him.

I yawned and said, 'I think I'll go back to my room to sleep.'

'If you want,' said Ella.

My failure to climb up to the window was still on my mind. 'I can be brave, you know,' I said. 'I'm not a coward.'

'I know that,' said Ella. 'You've been braver than anyone about Dad going.'

Maybe Ella was just being kind, but it seemed as if she really meant it, and for the first time in months and months, I believed I'd got something right. It was just a pity Dad wasn't there to see it.

Sixteen

It was raining on the morning of my birthday. It seemed like a bad omen, but I persuaded myself that it didn't mean anything. As I got up, I listened for Dad, hoping to hear his knock at the door. He'd come in with an armful of presents, all for me, saying that of course he wouldn't miss my birthday, it was unthinkable, and he'd travelled for miles just to be there. My birthday, November the eighteenth, would magic him back, I was sure of it.

But when I sat at the breakfast table with only Ella and Jude for company, I began to realize that the day might not go as I'd planned it. No Dad, no London Dungeon, no presents. I sat there, stony-faced so no one would know how much I minded.

Jude said, 'Look, I made you a card.'

She'd painted a picture of a mouse performing on a trapeze – or at least, that was what it was supposed to be. I tried to look grateful, but I'd wanted a bought card. I'd wanted a lot of things.

Ella had made one too. Ella's good at drawing, though I'm better for my age. She'd done some flowers on a window-sill and painted them and everything. I remembered the card Mum had given me on my last birthday. It had also had flowers on it and a rhyme inside about how lovely it was to have a daughter like me. We laughed about it because I wasn't exactly the goody-two-shoes daughter of the poem, but Mum said she meant all the words just the same. She wouldn't be without me no matter what.

We did the usual things, all with half our attention on the front door. We watched television and played games which Ella and Jude let me win because it was my birthday. For dinner we had chocolate sponge, with real dairy cream. I felt a bit sick, but I didn't say anything because it was meant to be a treat.

Ella said she wanted to clean the house again, so I should take Jude to the park. On your birthday, you never did any cleaning or washing-up, it was a family rule, so I took Jude off with the minimum of grumbles. Maybe Dad would be back when I came home.

Jude went on the swings while I stared at the ducks in the pond. It was a cold day, but then it always was cold on my birthday. Once, it had snowed. Normally, we were all at school. Mum had always baked a cake which I'd taken in to share at break-time. It was always the same: chocolate sponge with vanilla icing on the top and Happy Birthday Bessie in pink writing. Dad would pick me up after school and there would be a trip to see a film or to the bowling alley – my choice. Then, the weekend after, I'd have a party and invite eight friends. We'd go to McDonalds.

This year wasn't like that at all. It was stupid to

make comparisons, because you only felt like crying, and what was the point of that? I sat on the swing next to Jude's and went as high as I could. It was scary but nice too. I was almost as high as the tree-tops. I let the swing slow down, and eventually my heels scuffed the ground. I whooshed down the slide after Jude and my feet caught her in the back. She started to whine and then remembered it was my birthday and that she had to be nice to me.

The rain was barely noticeable now, but the seat of my jeans was wet from swinging and sliding in the damp. 'Can we go home now?' said Jude, blowing on her hands to keep them warm.

'Whose birthday is it?' I asked sternly and she subsided.

'If you wanted to go home I wouldn't mind,' she said, after a few minutes.

It seemed mean to keep her out just because I was scared to go back. What if Dad wasn't there? I knew Ella was cleaning so that the place would be ready for him. She was trusting in his return as much as I was. But I couldn't shake off the feeling that my twelfth birthday was going to be unlucky, so I told Jude we'd stay out a little while longer.

It was almost dark when we returned. I ran up to the front gate with Jude a few yards behind. The hallway looked bright through the frosted glass panel beside the door, and I thought I could see paper streamers and a balloon hanging up. Dad was home. He'd come back because of me, because it was my birthday. I ran into the house.

Ella came out to meet me.

'Where is he?' I said.

'He hasn't come yet,' said Ella.

I pointed to the balloons. 'Then who did this?' I said.

'It was me. I wanted you to have a proper birthday.' Ella looked pleased with herself.

'I thought he was home,' I said. I stormed into the living-room. 'Why did you make me think he was home?'

'I'm sorry,' said Ella in a small voice. 'I didn't think of that, I thought you'd know it was me.'

'How could I?'

Ella just stood there, hopelessly. I wanted to be nice to her but I couldn't, I felt too twisted up inside. 'This is the worst birthday ever,' I said. No presents. No outings. Nothing. And worst of all, no Dad.

Jude pushed her way on to my lap. She lay there with her head on my shoulder. 'Don't be sad, Bessie,' she said. I didn't push her away. Ella came and sat on the other side of me. She held my hand. It was getting darker and we hadn't put the light on in the living-room. It was funny, being slumped there in the half-light, but we didn't know what else to do.

Then Ella said, 'We did get you something. We were just waiting for Dad.' She hesitated some more, obviously not sure whether to carry on waiting or not. She looked at me, wanting me to tell her what to do.

'He isn't coming,' I said.

'No,' she answered. We sat there some more. After a while, Ella said, 'I'll get the presents, then.'

Jude followed her out. They came back with three parcels, neatly wrapped in purple patterned paper. They put them on my knee. I picked up the first one. I ran my fingers along the Sellotape and then prised off the wrapping. It was a purple T-shirt.

'I couldn't get a sweatshirt, we couldn't afford it, not knowing how long the money will last. But it's all right, isn't it?'

I could tell that the T-shirt had been bought off one of the stalls down the market. It was faded a little in the front, and the stitching was coming away at one of the seams. But at least Ella had thought about what I might like. At least she'd tried. I swallowed all my criticisms and did my best to remember that.

Jude said, 'Open this one,' and she gave me a flat parcel. It took me ages to unwrap it; half a roll of Sellotape had been used. It was like pass the parcel. Inside, there was a big bar of chocolate.

'It's all for you, you don't have to share,' she said.

'Thanks,' I replied. To tell you the truth, I was sick of chocolate. What I dreamed of now was proper food: roast potatoes, meat and two veg and not a cake or a chocolate bar anywhere in sight. But I gave Jude a hug and tried to be grateful. In the old days, it would have been one of my best presents. Jude wasn't to know that things had changed.

'The last present's from both of us,' Ella said. I undid it quickly. I wanted to get this present giving over with; I've never been a great pretender. I stared at the gift that was nestling in the crumpled wrapping. It was Ella's watch. I turned it over, hardly able to believe it. 'You want me to have this?' I said. It was Ella's pride and joy, she'd got it on *her* twelfth birthday and she'd hardly taken it off since.

'Yours doesn't work any more.'

'But it's only the battery. You could just have bought me one of those.'

'I wanted you to have a proper present,' Ella said, 'the kind Mum and Dad would have given you.'

I didn't know what to say. Jude looked at me in concern. 'Don't you like it?' she said. 'It's a new strap. I chose it. I got red because it's my best colour. Ella said if I chose the strap it could be from me too.'

'Thanks,' I said.

'Put it on,' said Jude.

I fumbled with the fastening, so Ella did it for me. Then she said, 'There's a tea. I did a special, nice one.'

We went into the kitchen. There were more balloons, and a cracker beside each of four plates. Ella picked up the extra one and put it by the sink. There were only going to be three of us. There was no point in pretending.

'I did proper food,' said Ella.

I could smell it. Grilled chops and mashed potatoes with carrots and peas. It was like Mum used to make.

'We shouldn't eat junk all the time,' said Ella. 'We'll get ill.'

I nodded and helped myself to the mash. 'This is more of a treat than birthday cake,' I said.

'I did it while you were out, and kept it warm in the oven.'

'Thanks,' I said.

We ate quickly, the way we'd done when we'd been with Carl and Shirley. For pudding there was a banana each. I'd never imagined preferring fruit to birthday cake, but Ella had got it right.

'We're going to have to try to eat proper food every day,' Ella said.

I nodded my agreement. I don't know why, but it was still hard to talk. I wanted to ask how much money was left. The balloons would have cost, and the chops, and the watch strap. Proper food would be expensive, most likely. I'd been looking in shops and adding up the cost of things. I hadn't realized how much money you needed just to eat. I began to understand then why Dad had fussed about money so much. I'd thought he was just being mean.

I offered to help with the washing-up, though I'd already guessed that Ella wouldn't let me. You never wash up on a birthday. We played Monopoly then, and I won, of course. You never lose on a birthday either.

I don't know why but I was tired. I wanted to go to bed. I looked at the clock. Ten fifteen. He wasn't coming then. I knew he wasn't but I still hoped.

Upstairs in bed, I held my watch up to the moon-light and looked at the dial. I remembered the chocolate, the balloons, and the purple T-shirt. I tasted the chops again. It was funny about Ella. She was changing. She was kind. She'd given me this watch. But Ella had always been kind, so it wasn't that. She was tougher, perhaps. She didn't agree with everybody all the time any more. She wasn't such a pushover. And she was braver too – she'd climbed that drainpipe. And then it occurred to me that maybe I was the one who'd changed. I could like Ella now in a way that hadn't been possible before. It was strange.

Seventeen

When Dad hadn't shown up on my birthday, it had confirmed my worst fears. Something *must* have happened to him. OK, maybe it was my fault, maybe he did go off because of me, because of the things I said, but I didn't believe that he was staying away just to punish me as I'd first thought. For one thing, he would have been punishing Ella too, and Jude, and they hadn't done anything wrong. And for another, even though he had moods, he'd always cared about us deep down. Look at how he'd protected us, how he wouldn't even let us out because he thought that London was too dangerous. I'd thought that proved he didn't care about us, but now I decided it meant that he did. He wouldn't have left us alone, facing all sorts of dangers, on purpose. He hadn't come home because he couldn't, not because he didn't want to.

Getting that straight in my mind helped in some ways but not in others. Maybe he still cared, that was good. But then it also meant that something had gone wrong, something that he couldn't help, which was bad. And how could me and Ella and Jude find out what it was? I turned it over and over in my mind and kept drawing blanks.

We needed to know. Gary was still sniffing

around, and if he found out what was really going on, he'd tell for sure, just to make us suffer. He was lurking outside when I went to buy some eggs for dinner, spying on us, trying to find out what our secret was. He followed me to the shop. As I paid for the eggs, he snatched them out of my hands, saying he'd drop them if I wasn't nice to him. Luckily, the man who owned the shop told him off and made him give them back, or we'd have lost our meal.

That was the other thing that was on my mind. We were very nearly out of money. The milkman had been knocking on the door, I'd seen him through the upstairs window. He was no longer leaving milk on the step. I suppose he was waiting for us to pay for the last lot. Once or twice in the past week, I'd got up very early and taken a pint off next-door's step. There didn't seem to be much choice.

There were other bills to pay too. Brown envelopes with windows and typewritten addresses kept coming through the door. Ella said they were demands for electricity and gas. If they weren't paid, you got cut off and then there was no light or heating and no way of cooking food. Maybe one of the bills was for water. We'd have the supply turned off, Ella said. We took to filling the bath with cold water every night, just in case. One time, I'd forgotten to turn the tap off and the water had overflowed, dripping into the kitchen through the ceiling. It had left an awful mess, but we carried on filling the bath anyway because being thirsty would be terrible. Just thinking about it reminded me of films I'd seen where people crawled through the desert with their lips cracking, seeing water shimmering in the distance but then finding it wasn't real, just a mirage, nothing more. I didn't want that to happen to us. But even as I thought it, I realized that everything was becoming like a mirage. Dad's return was starting to seem like that. I kept imagining he was there, sometimes even in the room with me as I tried to sleep at night. I didn't say anything to Ella, she'd probably think I was off my brain.

The big question remained though. What were we going to do? It was no good thinking we could last for ever without grown-ups, Carl had been right about that. But who could we tell? Carl and Shirley's mum and dad? They were the only people we knew here in London.

At that moment, I looked up and caught sight of Gary's face pressed up at the front-room window so that his nose was flattened and his nostrils were splayed. He traced two words on the misted glass with his forefinger and then ran off with a shout of laughter. I went and stood at the window. The words were back to front so it took a moment for me to decipher them. Then I realized it said WOGS OUT. I felt a rush of fury. I charged out of the house, determined to find him and to make him take it back, but he was nowhere in sight. Coward, I thought, he couldn't say it to my face, he could only scrawl it on windows. I went to rub the writing out but it had faded into nothing, so I went back indoors again, my legs shaking, more with anger than with fright. I wished I could ask Mum why we got called names. She would have known. Dad always said we should ignore it, but Mum knew that was hard because it had happened to her when she was young, and even when she was grown-up, sometimes she'd told us about it. Everything seemed so much more scary now that she was no longer there.

Ella came in. 'What's up?' she said.

'Nothing,' I answered. 'I was just wondering about Dad.' There wasn't any point in telling her about Gary. What could she do? It seemed better to keep my fears to myself. I was twelve now, nearly grown-up.

'It's not long till Christmas,' Ella said, sitting down beside me.

'It's ages away, almost a month.'

'A month isn't so long. Supposing he isn't back by then?'

'He will be,' I replied, sounding as if I really believed it.

'We might have to tell someone, Bess.'

It was as if Ella had been reading my thoughts. Or maybe it was just so obvious that this couldn't go on for ever that we couldn't pretend any longer.

'Who could we tell?' I asked. 'Shirley and Carl's mum?'

'I don't know,' Ella said.

We fell silent, and just thought about it. Then I said, 'If only we knew where Gran lives.'

'But we don't know, do we?' said Ella.

'We know roughly. I mean, we know it's Clapham because Mum always talked about it. And we know what the house looks like, because I remember it from the times we visited when we were young. If we could find her, she'd help us, I know she would, and she wouldn't tell anyone, especially not the police.'

'But where in Clapham could we look? How do you even get to Clapham from here? It's quite a big place. What'll we do? Scour the streets until we find a house that looks like the right one?'

'At least it's a start, knowing it's Clapham, it's something to go on.' And then it occurred to me. It was so obvious. 'Ella, Mum used to write to Gran all the time. She used to send her cards and presents at Christmas. There must be an address written down somewhere, there must be. Remember the boxes with the photographs? Dad took them down to the cellar. There used to be some old address books in with that stuff.'

We called Jude and opened the door in the kitchen that led downstairs to the cellar. We hadn't been in there since the week we'd moved in. It was bitterly cold and the bare bulb threw lots of shadows; even I found it creepy. Jude said, 'I don't want to be down here,' so we let her go back up again to play with her stuffed animals.

There were so many boxes still to unpack. They were heaped in unsteady piles like columns of building blocks. I took the ones on the right-hand side and Ella took those on the left. We began to go through them.

'Look at this,' said Ella, after a few minutes.

I hurried across excitedly.

'Sorry, it isn't the address. It's one of your old school record sheets. They weren't very impressed with you, were they?'

I lunged at Ella. 'Give it to me,' I said crossly. No one had the right to see that, only Mum. And she hadn't minded. She'd said I was an independent thinker and she didn't want me to change.

Ella subsided and handed it over. 'I was only teasing you,' she said.

'You never used to tease.'

'Well, I'm getting older and wiser. You always teased me.'

It was true, I had teased Ella a lot once. She'd been such a soft target. I lifted another box off the tottering pile and rummaged inside it. 'Are you planning to change any more?' I said.

Ella looked puzzled. 'What do you mean?'

'Well, it's just that you're sort of OK now, not too soft and not too hard, but I wouldn't want you to get any worse.'

'I'll bear it in mind,' said Ella drily, but then she smiled at me.

We continued to sort through the many boxes. My back started to ache with all the lugging and bending. Ella went very quiet, and I knew she'd found the photos of Mum. I didn't say anything to her. It's better to think your own thoughts when something like that happens, uninterrupted by anyone else. I found lots of old bills and a receipt for a carry-cot that was bought the year I was born. I was sure it had been mine and I was kind of touched that Mum and Dad had kept a record of it. On the other hand, I reasoned, they'd also kept a record of a load of brussels sprouts and cans of baked beans bought from the supermarket fourteen years ago, so maybe I shouldn't be too moved by their sentimental attitude. I stretched my legs out in front of me to stop myself getting cramp and my foot nudged an old exercise book labelled LOUISA GODDARD, CLASS 2A BROOKFIELD HIGH. It was from Mum's schooldays, then. Curious, I turned the pages. There, in big, loopy writing that was both like my mother's and very different at the same time, were several essays about life, the universe and everything. The teacher seemed to like Mum's work. It had got lots of ticks, and marks like 8/10 and 9/10. The comments ranged from interesting to sensitive and perceptive. I'd known in my head that Mum had once been a child of my age, but I'd never thought before about what sort of kid she'd been or if we'd ever felt the same. The strange thing was, she'd been very like me then, except that her compositions had been a whole lot better and spelt properly. Still, school was like that in the old days. Then, they'd put a lot of emphasis on grammar and proper spelling.

I read the first essay. It was called 'Things I Dislike'. In it, Mum described a boy, very like Gary, who called her lots of ugly names because she was from the Caribbean. I read it very carefully. She described how angry and hurt she'd felt, but she also said that if she'd really let it get to her, then the boy would have won because he'd said those things to make her feel sad and as if she didn't belong. That made sense to me. I stuffed the exercise book up my sweatshirt to hide it from Ella. I would show her eventually, of course I would, but for now, I wanted to keep it to myself. It was a way of remembering Mum and what she was like, a way of having her back again, I guess.

Jude came to the top of the cellar stairs and said it was tea-time and she was hungry. I went up to give her some spaghetti hoops on toast – it was my turn to cook that day. When I got back down, Ella was still sorting through the boxes. She sat back on her heels and looked at me in despair. 'It's like looking for a needle in a haystack,' she said. 'We don't even know if Dad kept Mum's address books. He might have chucked them out.'

This was true. We agreed to carry on searching till bed-time. I just couldn't give up the idea that we'd find Gran's address. I was certain that she would get us out of the mess we were in.

We had tea ourselves, and then we continued to look. We must have gone through thirty or more boxes apiece, sifting through meaningless bits of paper that should have been scrapped years ago. I decided that when I grew up, I wouldn't be a hoarder. Everything would go in the bin as soon as it was no longer useful.

'Oh yeah,' said Ella when I told her. 'Like your orange dog with the matted fur that you were sick on when you were eight. Or the book about witches that's missing the last five pages. Or –'

'Yes, OK,' I said, 'point taken, you don't have to go on and on. Did you find anything interesting, anything of Mum's?' I added, changing the subject.

'Nothing much,' said Ella, which I took to mean *yes, but I'm not going to share it yet.*

'Let me see it some time,' I said, and Ella smiled at me because she knew then that I'd found something too and that we both felt the same about Mum's things.

We were still searching well after eleven. Ella had put Jude to bed and come back down again. I was crying when she found me, tears of frustration and crossness.

'It's got to be here somewhere,' I said, 'I absolutely know it's here! I hate all this, I hate it, I just want it to be over!' I kicked one of the piles of boxes and they slid down with a crash. My crying became even noisier.

Ella sat beside me on the floor. 'Maybe it's here and maybe it isn't, but we can't find it. It's a waste of time. Don't worry, Bessie, we'll sort this out one way or another, really we will.'

I blew my nose. Ella was back to being motherly and I was glad. I'd never have admitted it, but surprisingly, I'd missed Ella's fussing and her kindly bossiness, and this time she wasn't being nice just because it was my birthday and she felt obliged.

'Welcome back,' I said.

Ella eyed the boxes that I'd just kicked over. 'Welcome back yourself,' she said.

Eighteen

I rushed into Ella's room next morning yelling, 'It's all right, I know how we can find Gran's address!'

Ella looked at me sleepily. 'How?' she said.

'The phone book. She's on the phone. We just have to look her up, that's all.'

Ella scrambled off the bunk. She pulled on her clothes hastily.

'Aren't you going to wash first?' I said.

'Can't wait,' she answered.

I looked at her in surprise. Ella was usually so slow and deliberate. Jude woke up and said, 'Are we going out?' so we explained that we were planning to find a phone box and check in a directory for Gran's address.

We hurried out of the house in a state of excitement. At last, there would be an end to being on our own. Before all this, my big wish had been to be in a world where there were no grown-ups to nag you, and where you could eat what you wanted when you wanted and go to bed whenever you liked. I was suddenly afraid. Now both Mum and Dad were gone. Maybe someone, somewhere had granted my wish.

All three of us fought our way into the phone

box at the same time. We jostled for position. And then I noticed. No phone books.

I felt weak with disappointment. 'It's all right,' said Ella, 'we just have to think calmly. Where else could phone books be kept?'

'I don't know,' I said flatly. 'If only we had our own phone. You get phone books automatically then.'

Relief filled Ella's face. 'Carl and Shirley are on the phone. They'll let us use their phone books.'

Of course. The answers to these things were so simple as long as you didn't panic.

'We'll have to wait until they get home from school,' said Ella.

For the next few hours we sat around the house, too jumpy to settle to anything, just counting the minutes. Because we were worried, we squabbled a lot, and Jude bawled constantly. I went outside and paced the street, past caring about truancy squads and any other dangers that might befall us. At five to four, we set off at a slow pace. The excitement was gone and we were afraid of disappointment.

Shirley answered the door and we explained what we wanted. She led us to the phone in the front room where Carl was sitting, reading a computer mag. He looked pleased to see us, or rather to see Ella, but she was too anxious about Gran to give him more than a friendly glance. She opened the book at G and ran her thumb down all the Goddards. Gran's first name was Elizabeth. I was named after both her and Bessie Smith, who was a blues singer. There were lots of E. Goddards, and two were in Clapham.

'Which one?' I asked.

'Ip dip . . .' began Jude. I frowned at her. It wasn't a game.

Ella rang the first one. A man answered. He told her to get off the damn phone and stop bothering him. Ella replaced the receiver, looking shaken.

Gran was the second E. Goddard then – she had to be. 'I'll do the phoning this time,' I said. I got the ringing tone. Ella leant against me, straining to hear. But the phone just kept ringing and ringing. There was no one home.

'Don't put the receiver down, keep trying,' urged Ella, so I hung on and on, but still there was no reply. Then the phone went dead.

Carl came over. 'It just stopped ringing,' I said.

'It only lets you try for five minutes and then it cuts you off,' said Carl. 'Don't worry, it'll be all right in the end, you'll see. She's just gone out, that's all. It'll be all right,' he repeated.

Once, I would have believed him, but since Mum's accident I no longer saw the world like that. Some things weren't all right, no matter how much you wanted them to be.

'We'll have to try again later,' said Ella wearily.

We decided to go to the shops to pass the time. As we went up the road, I noticed that Carl was holding Ella's hand. I nudged Shirley and she started giggling. 'How could anyone fancy Carl?' she said in a sisterly fashion. 'If she knew him like I do, he wouldn't see her for dust. Do you know

179

what he did the other night? He made me miss a really good film so he could watch *football*.'

'I like football,' I said. 'I used to support Leeds United.'

'I think it's rubbish,' said Shirley huffily. It was our first disagreement.

I was keen to keep the peace, so I didn't say anything more. Now that things were so uncertain, I needed Shirley. I was a bit worried about this. I'm the sort of person who speaks her mind. Normally I don't care what people think, they can take me or leave me. And now, here I was, being pathetic and holding my tongue just because Dad had gone. It's odd how things like that can change you.

We mooched around Woolworth's and tried to be interested in the music section, but the suspense was making me want to cry. All I wanted was to hear Gran's voice at the other end of the phone, comforting me, telling me that it was over now and nothing bad would happen ever again. I told Carl I wanted to go back.

'It's too soon,' he said, you need to give it at least half an hour.'

'Why?' I demanded. 'She could have got home the minute I put the phone down. What's so good about half an hour?'

'I'm just being sensible,' said Carl in a superior tone. 'I don't want you to be disappointed again, that's all.'

What did he know about disappointment? I couldn't help myself, I started shouting at him. 'Why don't you shut up? You talk like you're the one who's in charge of this, but you're not, it's me or Ella! If you don't shut up, I'll . . .' My voice trailed off. I couldn't think of anything that I could do to him right at that moment that he couldn't do back even harder.

Carl just grinned. 'I'm terrified,' he said.

'Don't laugh at me,' I yelled at him. The other Woolworth customers turned and stared.

'Don't be stupid and then I won't have any reason to.'

Ella suddenly cut in. 'Leave her alone, Carl. She's right, you are acting like you know everything, and you don't.'

I was caught completely off guard. Ella was defending me against Carl. I could hardly believe it. I smiled at her and she smiled at me and then we began to walk back. There was silence at first, and then Carl said, 'You know, I really do hope you find your gran.' He was obviously trying to make peace with Ella.

'We've got to,' she replied, 'or we'll get put in care. Dad's been gone for such a long time.'

I didn't look at Ella while she was saying this. I didn't want to believe it could happen to us. As we walked along the pavement, I suddenly had the sense that there was someone following behind us. I turned round sharply. Gary was standing there. 'What do you want?' I said to him. 'Why can't you leave us alone?'

He began to laugh. 'Told you I'd find out what's going on. Your dad's done a bunk and left you all by your little selves.'

'No he hasn't,' I said.

'I heard what she said to that boy,' he answered, pointing at Ella. 'My dad'll get the social on to you, and they'll send you all back where you came from.'

'You don't know what you're talking about,' said Ella, but he only laughed some more at us.

I wanted to hit him. I ran towards him with my fists clenched, but he held me at arm's length. I must have looked ridiculous, flailing the air, and after a while I no longer struggled and let my hands go limp. He gave me a sharp smack on my cheek. With watering eyes, I retreated. Fists were useless, I was coming down to his level. Anyway, he was bigger than me.

We went back to Carl's house and tried the phone again. There was still no answer and it was getting late. We had to go home.

That night, I dreamt of wolves. They were running in howling pursuit of us. Their faces kept changing. One of the big wolves looked like Dad. Then it looked like Gary. But worst of all, sometimes it looked like me. Then the house flew away, as if it was made out of paper.

Nineteen

It was just after 9 p. m. and I was examining a battered A-Z of London. We'd tried to phone Gran three more times that evening, but still there was no answer. Now that Gary knew we were on our own, we had to get out of the house, before he or his father contacted anyone official. We'd decided to go to the address right now. We just hoped she'd be back by the time we got there.

We left as quietly as we could, trying not to attract too much attention to ourselves. We didn't talk much; we were each too engrossed in our own worried thoughts. It was the coldest of nights. Our shoes scrunched the frost underfoot.

Carl had told us there was a bus that went all the way to Clapham from the High Street. We had to wait ages. Jude kept saying how cold she was. I was cold too, but not from the weather. It was an inside cold, the kind you get when something big is going to happen.

The bus came. We stayed on the lower deck, too nervous to bother going upstairs. I remembered the journey to the hospital the day that Jude's fingers had got stuck in the door. It seemed like a lifetime away. And all the time, in the back of my mind, I kept wondering what would happen if Gran wasn't there. Maybe we'd got the wrong E. Goddard out of the phone book, or perhaps she'd moved out of Clapham in the last few weeks. Or maybe she was on holiday. Although it was November, I knew that people did go then. She might have gone skiing or something. I smiled; the image of Gran skiing was so comical. I tried to explain it to Ella, but it came out muddled so she didn't understand. It's hard to make your inside thoughts clear at times, though I was getting better at it than I used to be.

'This is our stop,' I said, 'I remember that church.'

We got off the bus, torn between dread and excitement. Jude trailed behind. 'I'm tired,' she said, 'it's very late now, isn't it?'

Ella took her hand and started to tell Jude a story to keep her mind off her tiredness.

'I don't want to hear about giants, I want *The Three Little Pigs*,' she said.

I told her to shut up and walked along with my fingers stuck in my ears so that I couldn't hear it. As we walked, I was worried that someone, a policeman perhaps, would notice that we were out on our own so long after bed-time, but there were no police in sight, so after a while I calmed down a bit.

As we followed the map I'd sketched, I began to get excited. I recognized the toy shop and the school on the corner. I said this to Ella and she mumbled something back. I had to remove my fingers to hear her.

'Are you sure you remember them?' she repeated. 'You don't just think you do?'

'I remember,' I said, though she'd sown the seeds of doubt. Maybe I just wanted to recognize the landmarks so much that I actually thought I was.

E. Goddard lived in Denver Street and it was the next turning left. We quickened our pace. As we rounded the corner, I knew that we were in the right place. I began to run.

'Wait, Bessie!' Ella called, but I couldn't wait, all I wanted was to see Gran.

I reached the door. I pounded it with my fists, calling her name, banging and banging so hard that it seemed that the force might knock the house down.

And then suddenly, just when I thought there was nobody there, the door opened slowly, and there was Gran, standing small and bewildered in her nightie, wiping the sleep from her eyes. 'Gran,' I cried, tumbling into her arms. She fell back against the wall, and I had to steady her. And then Ella was there and Jude and we all were crying and talking at once and Gran was holding each of us in turn and telling us that everything was going to be all right, and I wanted to believe her so much but I couldn't just then, even though I wanted to.

We went inside the house and she made us cups of tea. Then she put some bacon in the pan and cooked it with tomatoes and fried bread. We were still crying a little.

'We've been phoning and phoning,' I said. 'Why weren't you home?'

'I'm sorry,' said Gran.

Ella nudged me to be quiet. 'It's OK, Gran, you weren't to know,' she said.

'Usually I'm here, but I had tea with a friend and then when I came home my leg was paining me so I took some pills and went straight to sleep. I don't hear the phone so well any more.'

'Gary says he's going to tell so we had to find you,' I said.

'Where's your father? And who's Gary?' she asked.

When we'd arrived on the doorstep I'd said everything in such a muddled way that Gran hadn't understood, so I explained again. Ella chipped in every now and then, but Jude just sat there, half asleep, playing with the china dog ornament she'd found on the sideboard.

'How long have you been alone?' asked Gran, when things made sense to her.

We weren't exactly sure. Ella knew the date we'd moved and I could remember when we'd seen Gran at the hospital, but after that, even though we'd looked at the newspapers, so many days had seemed the same that we couldn't separate one from another.

'A long time,' said Jude.

For a while, we were silent, each thinking, I guess, about that time. Then Jude said, 'I have to go to the toilet,' and that broke the tension and I took her off to give Ella the chance to see Gran by herself. It seemed only fair because she was the oldest.

When we came back down, Ella was in the middle of telling Gran how kind Carl had been. Gran asked if he was her boyfriend and Ella blushed and said, 'No, of course he isn't, how could he be?' and Gran replied, '"Methinks the lady doth protest too much."'

Jude said, 'What does that mean?'

So I answered, 'It means that Ella likes Carl a lot.'

Ella nudged me and I nudged her back, and we scuffled in a friendly way in Gran's living-room.

Gran's flat was smaller than I remembered it, but it was cosy and warm. Looking round at the pale green walls, and at the photographs of Mum and Dad and us when we were small, I began to feel safe. I'd almost forgotten what that felt like. I wished I could stay there for ever and ever.

Gran said, 'What we have to do now is find out where your father is.'

'How?' asked Ella.

'I'll ring some hospitals. Then if there's nothing, I'll contact the police.'

Ella looked scared. 'You think something's happened to him, don't you?'

Gran sat down with us at the table. 'I think that something's stopping him from coming home. He wouldn't have left you by yourselves unless he had to.'

'That's what I thought,' I said.

Gran gently stroked my arm. 'Whatever happens, you've always got me. I want you to remember that. I didn't see much of you all when Lou was alive because it was such a long journey. And then when she died I kept away because it was easier for me to blame your father than to think about how much I missed her.' Gran struggled to her feet. 'Still, there's no point in dwelling on the past. The important thing is the future. I have to make those phone calls.'

It took a long time. I amused myself by exploring the flat. It was too small for four people, I decided. We wouldn't be able to live there with Gran – there was only one bedroom. I picked up some of Gran's toiletries. She didn't have Feel Good, with its blond, blue-eyed models on the packet, she had conditioners for Afro-Caribbean hair and moisturizers and activator gel. She'd know how I could stop my hair frizzing out of control. In fact, there were lots of things that Gran would be able to tell me. I put everything back where I'd found it and was again aware of how little the flat was. If Dad couldn't be found, Gran would have to move in with us, and maybe she wouldn't want to. Some of my relief went and was replaced with uncertainty.

Then Jude shut herself in the bathroom and said she wasn't coming out, she was staying there for ever and ever and never going home. Ella got Gran off the phone but it took ages to convince Jude that if we did go home, it wouldn't be the same, there'd be someone to look after us. Eventually, Gran went back to her phone calls.

When she returned to the living-room, she looked upset. My heart started to beat very fast. I wanted her to tell us what she'd found out, to get it over with. I sat beside her on the edge of my seat, not sure I would be able to bear the news that anything terrible had happened to Dad, or that he'd died too, like Mum.

'He's not hurt,' Gran said, 'that's the first thing.'

Ella had been looking down at the table. Now she looked up hopefully.

'But,' Gran continued, 'he's not so well either. He's in hospital.'

Ella and I both spoke at once, trying to find out what was wrong. Jude's voice rose above ours. 'Is it flu?' she asked. 'He had flu before, at home.'

'Has anyone ever told you about the depression your dad gets?'

I nodded.

'Is it that?' asked Ella. 'Is that what's wrong with him?'

'Yes,' said Gran. 'He was found wandering the streets by the river. He seemed upset so he was taken to hospital. He didn't say much. He hasn't been able to tell anyone anything except that his name is Stephen. No one knew about you or that you'd been left alone. Your dad couldn't tell them, though they knew he was very worried about something. I expect it was that.'

'Will we all be going home soon then?' asked Jude, looking wary.

'Not for a while. Not until your dad's much better.'

'We can't stay here though, can we? It's too small,' I said.

'You won't be on your own, you'll be with me,

I promise. I haven't worked out how we'll manage it yet, but we will, and that's the honest truth.'

I nodded. There was something very safe about Gran. She wouldn't let us down, I was sure of it.

It was midnight before we got to bed, but I still couldn't sleep. We were all in the double bed in Gran's room, while she was on the sofa. This didn't seem right, but she'd assured us that she would be comfortable. I kept thinking of her leg and doubted this, but there wasn't anything I could do. Eventually, I got up again and went downstairs. I didn't mean to wake Gran, I just wanted to make sure that everything was still all right, but as soon as I came into the living-room she turned on the light. I went and sat beside her on the sofa.

'What is it, Bess?' she said.

'Nothing,' I answered.

So then she said, 'Something's eating you. Is it about your dad?'

I nodded.

'Can't you tell me what it is?'

I shook my head and looked down.

'Come on, Bess,' she coaxed.

I opened my mouth to begin, but nothing came out. 'I can't tell you,' I said.

'Yes you can. You just take your time,' said Gran, and she waited silently for me to speak.

Eventually I said, 'It was my fault.'

Gran took my hand in hers. 'What was, Bessie?' she said.

'That Dad went. I made him ill. It was all because of me.'

'How could it have been because of you?'

'I quarrelled with him, Gran. I told him it was his fault about Mum.' I explained about the day Dad left, and how I'd gone on and on provoking him. Then I said, 'The trouble is, I still hate him in a way, you see. He left us on our own.' I wasn't crying but I wanted to. My nose was running.

'It's a horrible feeling, blaming people,' said Gran.

I nodded.

'It's especially horrible if you mostly blame yourself.'

I thought about this for a minute and then I said, 'Why did Dad argue with Mum and let her go out?'

'We all get angry with people and say things we don't mean and think we've driven them away from us. But that's not why accidents happen or people have breakdowns. We just think that because we need to understand, and thinking things are our fault or blaming other people is easier than thinking there isn't any explanation at all.'

'Is that what you think, Gran? That there isn't any explanation?'

She sighed. 'Not for your mother's accident. That was just one of those things. Some people think it's to do with God or some other thing, but I don't know, Bess, I think these things just happen and we have to accept that they do and get on with the rest of our lives. That doesn't mean forgetting or not missing someone, but it means putting aside guilt and blame and the terrible sadness that can bring.'

I was silent for a while and then I said, 'What about Dad?'

'It seems to me that no one on this earth could blame your dad more than he blames himself.'

I looked up at her and knew she was right. 'Would it help if I forgave him? Forgave him properly, I mean?' I wasn't so angry any more, not really. More than anything I was sad, sad about him and sad about Mum.

'It wouldn't do any harm to forgive your dad, but first and foremost, he needs to forgive himself.'

'Would that make him well enough to come home?' I asked.

Gran nodded. 'I think so,' she said.

I didn't understand everything that Gran had told me just then, but somehow it made a difference. I suddenly saw that you could be angry with someone but still love them. I loved my mum. And deep down inside, I knew I still loved Dad.

I went back to bed, and snuggled down beside Ella and Jude. I listened to their steady breathing and tried to time my own so it matched theirs. There were no bad dreams that night, and I knew that our house would be safe from the wolf.